ANOTHER DAY IN PARADISE

Another Day in Paradise

A novel
by

JOSEPH SNEVA

Adelaide Books
New York/Lisbon
2019

ANOTHER DAY IN PARADISE

A novel

By Joseph Sneva

Copyright © by Joseph Sneva

Cover design © 2019 Adelaide Books
The cover art by Feliks Kaparchuk, (Instagram: @colorbyfeliks)

Published by Adelaide Books, New York / Lisbon
adelaidebooks.org

Editor-in-Chief
Stevan V. Nikolic

For any information, please address Adelaide Books
at info@adelaidebooks.org

or write to:

Adelaide Books
244 Fifth Ave. Suite D27
New York, NY, 10001

ISBN-10: 1-950437-10-8
ISBN-13: 978-1-950437-10-8

Printed in the United States of America

For Mimi

Chapter 1

It's been twenty years almost to the day since my infamous trip, though it feels like just yesterday. Funny how some memories have no time stamp. While it was *actually* happening, it all seemed like such a blurry and incoherent shit show, stuck in a fog of forgetfulness and shortcomings, like a dream—or nightmare. But now, as I look back two decades later, it gets clearer and clearer every day, fitting those pieces back together again. This was just before the days of cell phones and social media, so I'm basing this off sheer effort of racking my brain. Let me begin the story with who I was, where I was, and what I was doing at the time.

I had just turned twenty-one and had been living in L.A. for the past few months. I grew up in northern Oregon, just outside The Dalles, on a farm. My dad is a fruit farmer and your typical Scandinavian man—honest, hardworking, humble, and quiet, but when you set him off, you awake a lion and better run for the hills. He and my mom own a ten-acre spread out in the country. My mom is your typical homemaker—joyfully singing gospel hymns as she bakes her hundredth tray of muffins for the day. I'm the youngest of three. My two older brothers, Scott and Torey, are identical twins. They both have families now and live on the east coast. Scott is in Pittsburgh and Torey near Syracuse. Sundays at church, Saturday barbecues, and sporting events were common occurrences in the Kershaw family growing up. My two big brothers were all-star baseball players, so we'd spend a huge part of our time in the warm seasons traveling all over the state, even as far as Washington and California. While it was fun growing up on a farm, I have to admit—my town was getting smaller and smaller the older I got and the culture—or lack thereof—where everyone knew everyone, was really starting to eat at me.

There are not many things better than summers on the Columbia River. There, we would build bonfires and sip cheap beer on mid-July nights under the giant black canvas of infinity and her millions of diamond-sparkled stars glimmering, watching us. We would howl at the moon and live belligerent and free, with not a care in the world and our whole lives in front of us.

Well anyway, after high school I had zero drive and just bounced around from small job to small job. I had absolutely no ambition and every one of my weekends consisted of meeting with friends at the sand bar, and would drink until the sun came up. A couple buddies of mine moved down to the L.A. area right after graduation, to pursue their dreams of writing and directing movies. Out of the blue one day, they rang me up and asked if I wanted to come down and live with them just for the hell of it. It was not a difficult decision for me. Don't get me wrong, those mid-July nights until the sun came up were quite a hoot, but I began to notice my life was becoming a broken record.

So, with a few hundred bucks in my bank account, three or four bags of clothes in my car, and a fresh outlook on the future and all its' possibilities, I drove to the City of Angels, or the City of "Angles," as I like to cleverly refer to it as. It would take anyone in their right mind about five minutes in that fucking town to realize everyone there has an angle; something they want, and will try and get it no matter how cutthroat they have to be. Everyone operates with ulterior motives there and is either working on an angle, or looking for one. It's also true that it feels like not *one* single person is from there originally. It was always "girls from Ohio," or "boys from Kentucky," and yes, even a kid from Oregon. But I had to admit—I didn't hate it at first. I mean, does anyone really hate a city they've only been in for such a short period of time? And just like any other city, it has its pros and cons.

First the pros: gorgeous women, great food, amazing weather, beautiful beaches, wild nightlife, and you were able to see movies months before they were released into theatres anywhere else in the country, or the world for that matter. I remember coming home for Christmas one year and my hometown theatre had their first showing of a movie I can't remember the name of, but that's not the point. The funny thing was, I had seen that movie two months earlier in L.A. before it had been released nationwide. I got a kick out of that.

When you walk Colorado Boulevard in Pasadena, there are always people with flyers asking you if you would be interested in watching a screening of a new film. I always went to those. It's free admission and the only catch is that you fill out a simple one-page survey after the film ends. They were just general questions like what your favorite part was or asking you about your likes and dislikes or what scenes would you cut out, stuff like that. I enjoyed that. It felt a bit surreal to be a little ahead of the times, even if it was just for some stupid movies.

Now the cons: bad drivers, douchebags—who are also bad drivers—weather that is too damn hot, and those people—guy or girl—that say they know all these celebrities and that they have connections. They say they can get into all the hottest clubs and scenes. Those people are also called douchebags—guy or girl. Needless to say, L.A. has quite a few douchebags.

Anyway, so I had been living in L.A. for the past several months and working at this huge law firm in the downtown area named Wilson & Hammer. My buddy, Cole Harger—the guy who called me up and asked me to come down there in the first place—was the one who hooked me up with the job. He had told me on my drive down that the mailroom at the firm he was working at had a few openings and that he'd put in a good word. Well, his word must have been gold. I started working there within two weeks of arriving into sunny California. Cole was a great guy and a true friend. You really know you have true friend when someone will vouch for you at a job. I have to admit, back home when I was working odd jobs, I had some so-called "friends" of mine that would ask me if there were ever openings at my work and I would always lie and say no. The truth of it was they weren't really my friends. I knew they would be late all the time, fail a drug test, lie, or worse, steal something. When someone vouches for you for a job, you know you have a true friend. Cole was just a solid genuine guy anyway. He was a thick dude, with broad shoulders, hair always slicked back, and always wearing black, not in a creepy way, but in a classic rockabilly type of way. He loved listening to hard rock music and going to The Roxy and Whisky a Go-Go to see live shows. He was also a very talented musician in his own right, always playing very intricate guitar riffs on his acoustic around the apartment.

My first day at the Firm was a little overwhelming, to say the least. I mean, coming from a small farm town way up near the border of Washington State, and now smack dab in the middle of downtown L.A., amidst the millions of people heading to work, was making my head spin. The Firm was in a giant fourteen-story building in which they owned floors seven to fourteen. The mailroom, where I worked, was on the 7th floor. Even the entrance to the entire building was immaculate, with a long wide flight of stairs leading up to a courtyard that was beautified by a giant water fountain. It resembled something outside of a café in Paris, or better yet, some Roman temple. But who am I kidding, how would I know, I've never been to either of those places. So, once you pass the fountain you are twenty feet away or so from the main entrance, all the while walking on this gorgeous stone walkway. It was pretty amazing. As you open the doors, you first feel a huge gust of cold but refreshing wind. You see, back where I'm from you never go from hot weather into cold refreshing air conditioning inside. It's always the other way around. Back home I'd be outside cutting wood, helping my dad on the farm, or just at work doing something outside, and I come in and run my frozen fingers under scolding hot water, and *that* was refreshing. It hurts at first, kind of feels like stinging nettles, but feels good after a minute. It's the same kind of feeling in L.A. but opposite, if you get what I'm saying. In L.A., it could be ninety-two degrees outside in the middle of fucking January, and you are insanely sweaty and uncomfortable, especially in the dress shirt and tie that they had us wear for work. Not to mention, the heat bouncing off the pavement that would add another twenty degrees, I swear to God.

So anyway, I step inside to the cold refreshing air conditioning and the lobby is this giant unfurnished—but gorgeous—room with a ton of windows. The security station is in the middle and occupied by two men in suits, guys who couldn't make the cut at the police academy I assume. Like the security guards at Target stores, or better yet, mall cops. Guys like that always crack me up. To the right of the security station was a small food court, and just to the left were six elevators. It was a very busy area, but I was expecting that based on the fact that during my interview I was told that there were over two hundred employees at this particular firm. It was a big place. And it was exciting for me, if you want to know the truth.

I then followed the rush of people onto one of the elevators. It was like herding cattle. I asked someone to press the "7" button for me, as I was pinned back in the corner the moment the doors opened. Luckily, I was able to nudge my way through the bodies once the bell dinged for my destination. I stepped out onto the 7th floor, as did another guy. He was a fellow by the name of Jones, who also worked in the mailroom. His first name was Oly, but everyone just called him Jones. He was a skinny African-American guy in his mid-twenties, who stood almost six feet tall and walked in a kind of hurried strut that I found entertaining. His walk was legendary around the office. Most struts are slow and casual, but Oly Jones was one hyper dude. Everything he did was fast. He talked fast, walked fast, ate fast, worked fast, and smoked fast. He always smelled heavy of cigarettes as he smoked about two packs a day. He never had his shirt tucked in either, despite always being asked by our boss to tuck it back in. Jones had been working there for years, so I'm assuming all the higher-ups just figured it was a lost cause and let him keep his shirt untucked. Next to his strut, he was also known for his laugh. It was louder than hell. If he was told a funny joke, you'd be able to hear him cackle all the way in Ohio. He was always pulling little pranks on co-workers too, but nothing to piss anybody off. He was a really well-liked guy around the office.

"You the new guy?" he asked.

"That's me," I nervously but excitedly responded.

"Wuss yo name, my man??" Oly said. I replied with a fake confidence in my voice that I knew he could detect, judging by his big toothy smile and muttered giggles.

"My name's Quinn," I said. "Quinn Kershaw." Oly quickly responded.

"Welllll, welcome my man. You need any help with anything or anyone give you any shit you just hit me up, aight?"

"Right on, man. Thanks. Sounds good to me," I said. Jones smiled big as he always does and spoke sincerely.

"My name's Jones by the way. First name's Oly," he said, "but errybody 'round this muthafucka' jus' call me Jones." He held out his fist for me to bump, and I did.

"Sounds good," I said, as I nodded with a big grin and realized—I may have just met my first true friend from the area. Jones was a cool dude. He commuted every day from the Compton area and had a tough upbringing in a rough neighborhood. He told me months later that he had actually been shot once. The story goes: He and his friends were just chilling, shootin' the shit on his front porch one day, when a guy and his lady were walking by on the street. He and his buddies were acting a little foolish and started hootin' and hollerin' at the girl this guy was with, seconds later, the guy pulled out a handgun and starting shooting at them. They all ran through the front door and to the back of the house. After the debacle ended, Jones realized he had been shot in the foot and had to take a few months off work due to the injury. I always admired Jones for doing what he does—wakes up every morning from a bad neighborhood, takes a train, a subway, then a bus, all the way to work. He works until 6 P.M., then takes a bus, the subway, then a train, all the way back to his neighborhood. I truly admire Jones. He's a good guy, even though he's a damn Dallas Cowboys fan.

So, I follow Jones down the hallway as I have no idea where I'm going, and I quickly realize that the 7th floor isn't nearly as nice as the front entrance of the building or the lobby. It's not even close. It wasn't until later that day that I realized the 7th floor is strictly the mailroom floor. All the side rooms like the ones on the upper floors are used as offices for the attorneys. There on the 7th, they were just used for storage. Yup, we were the grunts. I didn't mind at all, though. It was all so foreign, grand, exciting, and brand new to me. Hell, I was just a farm kid, but now I was a man. I was a man in the City of Angels, or "Angles." Just a brief walk down to the end of the hallway beneath a flickering light stood Jones opening the door and welcoming me to the mailroom.

Somewhat of an organized chaos is what I observed at first. You had the whole department, five people in all, who were sorting incoming from plastic bins off the floor. Everyone was talking louder than hell, partly because of the stereo playing, and partly because they were just loud people in general. The stereo was on the far right counter by the fax machine. It was always set to Power 106, the local hip hop station. All that station ever played was Mariah Carey song after Mariah Carey song after Mariah Carey song, but never in that order.

The mailroom was full of characters. First, there was Shantel, a young single mother of two. She was from Portland, so naturally we hit it off being that we were both from the same state. Then, there was Carlos. He was covered in tattoos, but you'd never be able to notice due to him wearing his long-sleeve work uniform during business hours, then promptly throwing on an over-sized flannel that was buttoned all the way to the top the second 6 P.M. hit. Punk music was what he was all about. It was his life. It was in his blood. I'm pretty sure he went to twenty concerts a week, based solely on his V.I.P.

wrist bands and boozy breath. He actually knew the guys from the punk band The Deftones, and would hang out with them on the regular. Calvin was the lazy ass of the bunch. I swear he was duct-taped to his chair. He would literally roll around the room on that wheeled apparatus just so he didn't have to walk ten feet. He ate fast food like it was the last piece of gazelle meat fought over between two starving lions. For lunch, he would often pay for ours if we would go get his just so he didn't have to move. Nobody in their right mind can say no to a free lunch. If you do, you are either nuts or you work above Floor 7. Then there was Ronny. Ronny was an older dude around forty-five who looked about twenty-five on some days and eighty-five on others. He was short, bald, and overweight, and had his own language it seemed. When he wouldn't agree with you about something or get a little irritated with you, he'd call you a "Davey." Whatever the hell that meant. When he thought you were spot on about a particular subject, he would call you a "Diaper Dandy." A different kind of dude, that Ronny was. He was an old school hip-hop kind of guy and was always humming and rapping Rick James or attempting the high parts of "Tired of being Alone" by Al Green. Sadly, I heard that Ronny died of a heart attack last year. He was truly a "Diaper Dandy" and thinking of him always makes me smile. And of course lastly, there was Jones.

Everyone in our department was under thirty years old except for Ronny and our supervisor, Bill Fulton. Bill was a tall, goofy, middle-aged white guy, with a long grayish pony tail to his butt and an odd goatee, with the left side of it pure white and the right side of it completely black. It was the Holstein heifers of goatees. He had a strong lisp and was the king of one-liners too. If you ever asked how his day was going, he'd reply, "Ah, juth another day in paradithe." Or, if you asked him a question you'd know he would certainly agree with, he said, "Yeth thir, I'll drink to that!" One day, just for the hell of it, I wanted to test the waters. I walked over to his desk and asked him if I could use the restroom. We could obviously use the restroom whenever we damn well pleased, but I just wanted to hear what he'd say. And wouldn't you know it, he replied with, "Yeth thir, I'll drink to that." On weekends, he ran a charter fishing boat off Catalina Island. I have to admit, he always had good stories on Mondays about the tourists he'd taken out. Some of the stories were boring as hell, but others were funny and quite amusing. One of the mailroom favorites was of an old rich lady getting sea sick and puking off the side of his boat.

My job turned out to be easy once I got the hang of it. It was quite repetitive, actually. What job isn't, though? At the bottom of every hour I would take my empty cart and elevator up each and every floor and gather the outgoing mail that was set on the outbox of every secretary's desk. There were about fifteen secretaries on each floor, and each of them worked for two or three attorneys. I'd pick up the mail and bring it back down to the mailroom, then send everything through a huge automated stamping machine. I literally would walk each of the floors eight times daily. I must have met a couple hundred people in my first few days, easily.

It was a pretty wild place to work, with so many walks of life in one place. You had the gossip ladies on the 8th floor. There was Ada, Paulina, Sonja, and Janice. They loved nothing more than these three things: Bill Clinton, Oprah, and General Hospital. You always knew never to go into the lunch room from 11 A.M. to noon, unless you didn't care about what channel you watched while you ate. Those ladies had the T.V. on lockdown, and the only thing Ada, Paulina, Sonja, and Janice were letting you lay your eyes on was General fucking Hospital.

On the 13th floor, was a certain corner of young attorneys and secretaries who were always having birthday parties, drinking champagne in the morning, cracking dirty jokes, or talking about karaoke from the night before. They were always a fun bunch to stop by and chat with for a few minutes while I did my hourly mail runs.

I hated the 14th floor. The first outbox to collect there was from this secretary, Mary Chamberlain. She was an old hag who always had a scowl on her face and was in a bitter bitchy mood every single day. I actually felt quite bad for her. She was overweight and very unattractive, and she dressed awful. That aside, it was her attitude that made me not like her. She was the type that wanted to see people fail, so I avoided her at all costs.

My second week at the firm I fell in love, though it was terribly one-sided. She was an attorney, and her name was Ruth Yen. She was Korean-American with straight jet-black hair to the middle of her back. She wasn't much older than me—and yes, already an attorney—so I knew her looks weren't the only thing she had going for herself. Everything about her was amazing, especially her laugh. Her laugh knocked me out. She had this very high-pitched, breathy laugh, and when she opened her mouth to let out a giggle, there was always a little delay before any sound came out. It was adorable. And she always laughed at me when I was trying to be funny with her, which always drove me wild. She only stood about five foot one, but when I stood next to her waiting for the elevator, she was seven feet tall. And it killed me, she had a little bubble butt that stuck out when she walked, even without wearing heels. She was goddamn terrific. There was only one problem. You couldn't see into her office just by walking passed it since it was a corner office and the angle made it impossible unless you poked your head in, which would be a bit awkward, for her of course. One day, I noticed you could see her through a reflection off a framed picture on the wall that hung adjacent from her office door. So, five days a week, eight times a day, I would round that corner on the 11th floor, swoop by to pick up the mail off Tina Bertner's outbox, and take a quick glimpse of Ruth through the reflection off the painting. It always made my day, every day. One Friday night, when all of us co-workers were at happy hour, she drove me home. When she dropped me off I told her that I wanted to kiss her but probably shouldn't. Number one: I am an idiot for telling her I wanted to kiss her in the first place. And number two: I am an idiot for not trying.

Then there was the 9th floor. Oh, the 9th floor. This floor was occupied by a handful of likeable scoundrels that would one day change my life, for better or for worse. The infamous events would soon come to fruition, but for now it was just another day in paradise.

Chapter 2

Harvey Gans owned the 9th floor. Hell, he owned the whole Firm if you asked me. He was a senior partner, 51 years-old, or years *young* if you asked *him*, and had this magnetic quality about him that everyone gravitated toward. All the young up-and-coming attorneys wanted to be him, all the older near-retirement attorneys wanted his youth, and all the secretaries wanted to sleep with him. Everyone else just simply wanted to know him. He drove a black Mercedes which car model didn't officially come out until the next year. He was dating a cute attorney from the 14th floor, Colleen Paxon. Their relationship seemed awfully loose though, and Harvey took every opportunity he could to show that he was a young single man free of attachment and commitment. On any given day, you would see Harvey either around the office, waiting for the elevator, or across the street having lunch, and you would always see him surrounded by four younger attorneys. They were basically his assistants. He was their Robin Hood. Hell, he was their Jesus and they were his disciples. The apostles were: Paul Chance, Glen Patton, Rory Carson, and Barry Camaretti—all of them in their early thirties.

To tell you the truth, I did not like Harvey at first. He seemed extremely arrogant. Always walking around with his disciples acting like he was God's gift to man, or woman. Paul

Chance had told me a story once about Harvey flipping his lid days before a trial they were preparing for, cursing out Paul and the rest of his crew for being ill-prepared yada yada yada. Knowing that obviously didn't help the case toward my impression of him.

The first time I met Harvey Gans I was terrified of him. I was down in the mailroom feeding letters through the stamping machine, when Shantel walked up with a manila envelope and asked if I could drop it off at his office. It was urgent and she had just started her lunch break.

She explained, "Aight, if the door's open, just knock a couple times on the open door, and hand it to him. If the door is closed, just give it to his secretary. And if the secretary ain't there, just throw it away."

"Wait, what? I asked.

"I'm just messing with you dog, damn." Shantel was always playing around like that. I was new though, so it took a while for me to get her humor. "It's a joke bro," Shantel said. "Lighten up. Just throw it on his secretary's chair if she ain't there. Remember, the chair though, not her desk. The secretaries have so much paperwork and shit on their desk that they might not see it. Always set incoming mail on their chairs, you got it?"

"Okay got it, thanks," I said. I grabbed the manila envelope from her and hurried down the hall. Since Shantel had just explained to me that it was kind of an emergency, I took the staircase instead of the elevator.

There were six elevators in our building, but sometimes you would be waiting there for five minutes. That may not seem like a long time, but try just staring at a wall for five minutes. It feels like eternity. So, I hurried up the stairs, passing the 8th floor, and made my way to the 9th. I opened to door and turned right, heading toward Harvey's office. I noticed his door was wide open, and as I got closer I could see him working away with piles and piles of paperwork surrounding him. The stacks took over his office like some vacant cabin out in the woods somewhere, overrun by vegetation for hundreds of years, grass growing up through the wooden planks, tree branches broken through the windows that have made their way through the roof, and moss covering the inside and outside walls. I was now standing in his doorway.

"Knock, knock," I said. "I have this urgent letter for—"

"Just leave it on the goddamn chair for chrissakes!" Harvey yelled. He didn't even look up to see who he was talking to. He was having a terrible day, you could tell. He took off his glasses with one hand, then, rubbed the bridge of his nose as he squinted in either—fatigue, nausea, or stress. My guess was all three. Also on the desk sat a half-empty bottle of Crown Royal and a small empty glass with ice cubes in it. Yes, he was most certainly having a bad day. I set the manila envelope on one of the two chairs in front of his desk and left.

That was my first encounter with Harvey. I was pretty damn intimated from that moment on. I dodged him everywhere I saw him, though I don't think he ever knew that it was me who was in his office that day.

The ice was finally broken when Cameron from the Copy Department—who was also a grunt—Carlos, Jones, and myself all went out for happy hour at The Shadow Club. The Shadow Club was in the downtown district just blocks from the Firm, and it was an amazing establishment. Modeled after the prohibition era, it had this 1920's speak-easy-type theme. The entrance was in a dark alley and unassumingly there on the left, was the door. After you get carded, you walk in and notice a glass room—the smoking room. Decorated with leather couches, tons of tall exotic plants, and a couple high chairs in the back, you can get your shoes shined while puffing on a stogie. You then make your way down to the bar via the spiral staircase and you are then underground. Waitresses walking around as flappers selling cigarettes and shots of whiskey in light bulbs, not shot glasses, burlesque women performing on the stage to a live jazz band, vintage machinery and exposed brick as the décor, and a wild Friday night crowd—who are just as in awe as you are from the time machine of the establishment—is what awaits you.

We were all sitting at a table, enjoying the one-of-a-kind atmosphere, when Cameron threw some knowledge my way that I wasn't quite prepared for.

"We're gonna have to get a bigger table," he said, with a louder voice than usual. Cameron was a very soft-spoken guy. He was a humble kid who had moved to California from Chicago, not long before I made my way down there myself.

"How come?" I said. "It's just us four, we're good, dude."

"Nah, man," Carlos butted in, "Harvey's coming."

"Harvey Gans?" I asked. I was shitting my pants. Why the hell would he come and hang out with us? I thought to myself. Then I said it out loud. "Why the hell would Harvey Gans come and hang out with us?"

"Well, I need a ride home, don't I?" Cameron said.

I looked at him with squinty confused eyes, and could feel my left eyebrow slightly lifting as if I was telepathically letting him know that I did not understand what the hell he meant. Picking up on my confused look, Cameron explained.

"He's my dad."

"Who's your dad, Harvey? Harvey is your dad?" At the *exact moment* I asked him that, I studied his face and could detect similar features that he and his father possessed—pointy nose, thin lips, dark brown hair. "No way," I told him, with a straight face and in a beaten voice, as if I had just been conquered in a grueling ten-hour game of chess. "He flipped out on me one day," I said.

"Who did, my dad?"

"Yes, your dad!" I argued. Cameron seemed very surprised at my comment.

"What do you mean he flipped out? What did he do? What did he say to you?" Cameron asked. I started to tell him the story of when I dropped off that manila envelope to his office when Carlos and Jones interrupted us from across the table.

"Hey we're gonna go grab another drank, try and get some ladies too, ya know?" Jones hollered at us. It was louder than hell in there. "You fellas want anything?"

I looked down at my glass and noticed only a drink of beer left, so I threw it down with one gulp and shook it in the air at Jones letting him know what I had just done. "Jones, another beer for me!" I yelled out.

"I'll take another too!" Cameron called out. Jones and Carlos disappeared into the crowd toward the bar, when Cameron turned back towards me.

"Okay, so you dropped off an envelope at my dad's office and he yelled at you to put it on the chair?"

"Yes," I said, "exactly." Cameron looked at me shaking his head, and with this grin on his face as if I didn't know a simple math problem, like two plus two, and he was about to explain it to me.

"Quinn, you need to chill dude. Don't worry about it. It's not a big deal. He probably didn't even look up and notice who it was." Cameron wasn't trying to comfort me or make me feel better. He was being completely genuine, hell, who else would know how his father acted better than he would?

"That's exactly what else I was gonna tell you," I explained. "He didn't even look up, so I don't think he knows it was me. So he probably still isn't pissed at me, right?"

"Listen Quinn, these attorneys get stressed as hell. One day they are happy as a clam, cracking jokes and high-fiving each other. Other days, they're buried in paperwork and don't leave their offices for hours and hours. Yea, they make some serious bank, but we have it better in a lot of ways. They have better cars and bigger houses, but they also have a better chance of having a heart attack." Cameron laughed then acted out having a heart attack by grabbing his arm and gasping for air. "This case was just too damn stressful," he shouted out. "I'm guilty. I'm guilty your honor." He then gasped his last breath and laid he face on the table. He lifted his head after a couple seconds and turned toward me with his eyes crossed and a goofy smirk on his face. I was busting up. It was seriously comical. Cameron was never the one to want attention and be funny, but I think the alcohol was hitting him a tad hard that night.

For the next few minutes, Cameron and I sat back and surveyed the scene. The table to the right of us sat some pretty boring people. They were drinking wine and talking about a painting or something. I'm quite sure they were trying to be intellectual, but were just playing the part. Los Angeles has a lot of actors, on and off the screen, if you know what I mean. We noticed directly in front of us, two girls. One short one with black hair shaped right below her ears, her bangs cut straight across the middle of her forehead. The other girl was tall, red-haired, and skinnier than a pencil. They kept looking over at us giggling and whispering to each other, and every few seconds taking a sip off the straw of their mixed pink drinks.

"Is this go time?" I asked Cameron.

"Hell yea," he said, as he finished his beer. He had half of his drink left, but he gulped it down with a few quick swallows. This was no time for patience. "Let's do this. I got the redhead."

And wouldn't you know it. Right as we stood up to test the L.A. dating scene waters, two douchebags came up from behind them and started chatting their ears off. The girls turned back around to us with looks of desperation, hinting that maybe we should go and save them. But it was too late. The douchebags were in there deep, and "Bangs" and the "Red-headed Pencil" were swallowed up whole.

"Well good goin' you sons a' bitches." And there he was—Harvey. He was watching us the whole time. He unbuttoned the front of his million-dollar suit and sat next to me.

"Did you just see that?" Cameron asked his dad.

"Hell yea I did!" Harvey yelled. "This city always has these douchebag guys that come up and feed these ladies some bull-shit. They tell these aspiring small town girls about this or that, or 'Betty Lou from Kansas' how she's so pretty, how she could be a model if she wanted to, which they probably all want to too, that's the goddamn problem." I could not believe my ears. He was talking the same way I was thinking.

"What's your name kid?" Harvey asked me.

"Quinn Kershaw," I said, "I work in the—"

"Mailroom, right? Yea, I've seen you around. Listen," Harvey explained, "don't ever try and be a lawyer." He grabbed his son's beer off the table and took a giant swig, clenched his teeth, and let out a satisfied sigh from the taste of his beverage. "Being a lawyer sucks. You kids got it good. You are young, full of ideas. You kids got all this energy, being a lawyer just takes that all away." Again, I could not believe my ears. Was this re-ally Harvey Gans? Was this the same guy I was so intimidated by all this time, being scared he would see me around the Firm and flip out on me for the day I dropped off that damn manila envelope? I later told him about that envelope incident, and he could not recollect it at all. He was either lying about it, because he felt embarrassed, or he honestly did not look up that day from his desk and notice I was dropping off his mail. Either way, all my worrying was for nothing. "Tell you what guys," Harvey said to Cameron and I, "if you two go rescue those damsels in distress from those clowns, you Quinny, can have my credit card until we leave tonight. Any drink you want and for anyone you want. Just look at it this way—pretend those douchebag clowns are just dragons."

"Dragons?" I said.

"Yes, dragons. They are just dragons, but you're the dragon *slayer*. Look at it that way. Try it."

I studied Harvey's face to see if he was joking around, but he was as straight-faced as a judge, as he took another drink off Cameron's bottle of beer. He was a damn poet too, I thought to myself. It didn't take me more than a second to agree, since I was broke as a joke and those girls were awfully cute.

"Alright, you're on," I said, and Harvey and I shook hands. I didn't even wait for Cameron to get up from the table as I raced over to the dark-haired girl with bangs and gently tugged her arm. "Excuse me," I said. "What's your name?"

She looked at me with a look of shear thankfulness. I don't think the case was that she really liked me or anything. I just think her and her friend were not particularly amused by the guys that were hitting on them at that moment. She hadn't even said her name yet when I blurted out another question. "Can my buddy and I buy you and your friend a drink?"

"Excuse me champ, but we were talking to these fine ladies," one of the douchebag clowns said. I mean, I can't really blame him. If I was in his position I would've done the same thing.

"No, I'm sorry," the dark-haired girl told him. "Thank you for the chit chat, but we met these guys before you and we're gonna go have a drink with them." The two girls turned around and started walking back to our table when the other douchebag clown had to give his two cents.

"You girls are nasty, anyway," he said. It was almost comical. I mean, really? What a stupid thing to say. These girls were damn classy, and it didn't even bother them. They just blew it off and had big smiles on their faces as I pulled out a chair for the dark-haired girl, and Cameron walked around the other side to assist the redhead with her seat. As I sat down in my spot, I noticed in front of me a credit card. It read: "Harvey Gans." I looked over to Harvey, who was just to my right at the head of the table. He just picked up his beer, smiled at it, took a gulp, and finished it with a big satisfied sigh. This time I do not think it was because of the taste of his drink, but to the conquest of his new friend. That is how I like to think of it anyway.

The rest of the night was an absolute blast. A legit 4-piece jazz band was playing on stage, equipped with slick suits and the whole nine yards. We danced our asses off. They even had a song where they asked for a person in the crowd to come up and sing a small part of one of their songs. Well, Cameron was in awfully good spirits being that he was bouncing around the room off round after round of cocktails, with the dark-haired girl on his arm nibbling on his ear all night. It's important to note that about halfway through the night Cameron and I switched girls. Apparently, Leanne, the dark-haired girl, was from Chicago too just like Cameron. Once she mentioned that to us, he was all about her. I didn't mind, though. Courtney the redhead was cute too, but Leanne took the cake. So, finally, after a little bit of encouragement from us and multiple rounds of liquid courage, Cameron hopped up on a stage and danced around like Charlie Chaplin. It was legendary. He finally grabbed the mic and yelled, "I love whiskey!" Everyone in the crowd hollered, laughed, screamed, and cheered. It was epic, especially coming from such a humble kid like Cameron. He ran back toward the drums, then turned around and ran toward the crowd as if he was going to jump off and stage dive. He was just pulling everyone's leg, though. He sprinted to the edge of the stage and did a fake jump, off one leg, keeping his other foot planted, then stepped back and raised his arms in a "V." That got the crowd louder than hell. Everyone gave him a big cheer as a couple of the band members stopped playing their instruments mid-song and helped him off the stage. He was having a little trouble with his balance.

The evening continued with more dancing and more drinks. We never saw Jones or Carlos the rest of the night, though. I talked to them the following Monday at work and apparently, Jones got in an argument with a fella in the smoking room. He told me a guy started "talking shit," but when I caught up with Carlos at lunch he told me the guy said something about the Dallas Cowboys to Jones. If there's *one thing* you don't say to Jones, it would be talking bad about the Dallas Cowboys. That's just off limits. And when everyone's had a few rounds of loud-mouth soup, well, that doesn't help with the situation either.

We said goodbye to the girls around closing time and exchanged numbers. And although Cameron and I never did call them, nor them us, it was okay. Now they are just in my bag full of great memories. It always gives me a healthy smile thinking back to that night, when Courtney and I pretended to be in Dirty Dancing. I think she even called me Swayze for the rest of the night after that, or maybe I made that up in a dream.

I honestly can't remember. However, I do remember walking up to the bar to close my tab. It read: $263.47. Holy shit, I thought to myself. Harvey is not going to be happy. I then noticed out the corner of my eye that Harvey was standing next to me and looking over my shoulder at the tab. I was bracing myself to be yelled at once again, preparing myself for Harvey to tell me to put that manila envelope on his "goddamn desk," but he just sniffled his nose in a wise guy, snotty sort of way.

"Really? That's all you could drink? And you even had ladies you bought drinks for?" he said. "You have a lot to learn, Quinny boy. It's a good thing you have me around." I shrugged my shoulders and smiled.

"Yes, I suppose I do," I replied. Turns out I was wrong about Harvey. Harvey was a good guy and just a father who made a lot of money at a job he kind of loathed.

"C'mon, sign my name and let's get outta here," he said. When he walked back to our table to grab his coat, and as I started to sign the bar tab, I began to write the first letters of Harvey's name. I had a pretty good buzz going, so I squinted my right eye and tried focusing harder. I scribbled out the letters. I looked over at Harvey, then back at the paper, and finally signed the tab—in cursive—what his real name was—or what I thought it should be. I wrote—"The Dragon Slayer."

Chapter 3

I woke up the next morning with the sound of fast fingers tapping on plastic, and gunshot noises coming from the television. My two roommates were playing their video games as they always do.

Surprisingly, I wasn't as nearly hung over as I thought I'd be. I usually feel like crap in the morning from a night of debauchery, even nights with a lot less drinking too. I've been known to drink two or three beers when I'm out on the town, or even when I'm just at home eating dinner, and I'll wake up the next day dehydrated dry as a bone, with sore joints and my heart beat behind my eyes vowing never to have a drink again. It's a lot of fun.

But today I felt rather fine, though, I wasn't quite sure how I got home. The following Monday at work Cameron had told me he called a cab for me and that his dad paid the fare. I told him I'd pay Harvey back, but Cam just laughed it off explaining to me that his dad would never accept my money.

Cole and Terry played intensely on their "shoot 'em up" video game as I sat up from my bed and watched them for a few minutes. It wasn't really a bed, though. I slept on a cot against the wall in the living room of their two-bedroom apartment. It was a raggedy ole thing, but I didn't mind, and I never complained to them about my sleeping situation. It was a place to stay and I wasn't there much anyway. That is one thing about L.A. that I truly loved. There was *always* something to do.

Terry was another friend from my hometown. He was a grade below me, and we were more like acquaintances than friends. To tell you the truth, he really annoyed the hell out of me. He was a string bean of a guy with bushy red hair, freckles from head to toe, and a neck that resembled a giraffe's. He also had these yellow fingernails from smoking about fifty self-rolled cigarettes a day and blood-scabbed nubs from chewing on them. He had a crummy vocabulary to boot. More times than not, he would finish sentences with "and everything." For instance, if you said, "Hey, we should probably go get groceries tonight," he would reply with, "Yea, we are all out of milk and everything," or he'd say, "Good point, we need to get more food and everything." It definitely got on my nerves and Cole's too, I bet. The thing I just couldn't stand most about him was that he didn't have to work. Terry was a spoiled rich kid and his parents sent him money every month. Not sure how much he got, but I'm willing to bet it was more than I made in a month. And so Terry just bummed around the apartment day in and day out wearing his bathrobe and drinking his coffee in the morning with a dash of Bailey's Irish Crème, and sipping his rum and cokes throughout the rest of the day. I would always come home from work and he would be three sheets to the wind and acting like an ass. I never understood why he rolled his own cigarettes, though. They were the cheapest kind of smokes money could buy. He probably saw somewhere that Johnny Depp, or someone like that, smokes the *exact* same brand. Terry always thought he was big time, but he never left the apartment. He was an interesting fella and certainly one of a kind.

I finally stood up from the cot after realizing how uninteresting watching my roommates play video games was. I rubbed my eyes, stretched my arms out as wide as I could, then let out a great big yawn.

"Rough night?" Cole asked.

"Just a tad," I laughed. "Do you guys know what time I came in last night?" They both were still staring at the T.V. and laser-focused on the next criminal they had to shoot.

Terry chimed in, "Dude, you were singing some loud annoying song and everything. It was some hard rock crap or something. You woke me up, you shithead."

"Wow, really?" I asked. "So what time was it when I came in?"

"I don't know, two-thirty or something," Terry said.

"Oh chill," Cole said, as he laughed a little under his breath. "I thought it was funny." Cole paused their game and turned to Terry. "The song he was singing was Judy is a Punk by The Ramones, for your information." Cole always loved putting Terry in his place and it always ate at Terry when Cole, or myself, knew something that he didn't.

Just then, I realized that Harvey had told me something the night before, something of substantial significance and I couldn't seem to remember. What the hell was it? I tried retracing my steps from the night before, in my head, but was getting nowhere. I stood there zoning out at the wall thinking as hard as I could. It was like an itch I couldn't scratch, like those ones right in the middle of your back you can't reach and there isn't a savior in sight to scratch it for you.

"Hey Quinn, you okay? You look weird," Terry said, as he un-paused their game, both of them getting sucked back into shooting as many villains as they could, in the abandoned warehouse full of mafia goons their characters were snooping around in. I didn't hear a word he said though. What the hell did Harvey tell me last night that was such a big deal? I was forcing myself to think hard, but I had nothing. "Earth to Quinn," Terry said. He was really getting annoying now.

"Shut up Terry, I'm thinking," I barked at him. Ah, whatever, I'll figure it out sooner or later, I thought. Terry was reminding me of a fly that keeps buzzing around you, and you can't swat him dead. When he talks, that's when the fly is closest to your ear and you scrunch your face into your neck and rapidly brush away at your ear as you jump up and make your space between you and that annoying little creature. That's how I felt at that moment, so I decided to go grab breakfast. Luckily, I slept in my clothes from the night before. I even had my shoes on making it that much easier for a speedy getaway.

"I'm gonna walk up to Lucky Boy and get some breakfast," I said, as I quickly passed by the T.V. I honestly didn't want to interrupt them playing their game. They are quite serious about their "vids."

"Breakfast? Ummm, do you know what time it is?" Terry asked.

"Who cares, ya dumb son of a bitch," I heckled out to him, as my tipping point was near the max.

"It's one-thirty in the afternoon. Doesn't that mean you're getting lunch and everything?" Terry was such a schmuck.

"Dude, shut up. I'm hung over. Quit giving me shit," I said. I wasn't hung over, though. I felt pretty good, but I was so sick of that scab they call Terry, and if I could find any opening for him to be less of a pest I was going to go for it, and that opening was to go get breakfast.

"Later, Cole," I said, as I walked out and closed the door. I wasn't going to give Terry the satisfaction of a goodbye from me. It doesn't sound like a very big deal, but believe me, it ate at him for me only saying goodbye to Cole and that right there put a smile on my face.

I smiled all the way down the stairs until I felt a wet drop on my head, then my cheek, then a few drops on my shoulders. It was raining out—not a lot—but enough to wipe the smile off my face. I hated rain. I came to California to get away from it for chrissakes. Luckily, it wasn't raining that bad so I stayed the course and walked up the street to Lucky Boy.

My destination was just two blocks up and one block over from our apartment so visits there were quite often. It was an old-school mom and pop burger joint that had been around for decades. There was small dining area inside and a few picnic tables out front facing the road with a covered top. I'm pretty sure the roof of the outside eating area was made for people to dine in the shade from the unrelenting California sun, but today it was like being back at home. Today, that roof was now protecting the Saturday burger eaters from Heaven's nasty bathwater. I hated the rain.

I walked up the block with my head down and shoulders scrunched up to my ears. I never understand why I—and everybody else—always does that when it rains and you have no umbrella. It's not like that posture is going to keep you any dryer. But I still do it, as does everyone else.

After my grueling three-block walk, I made it up to the order window at Lucky Boy. The only thing I hated about that place was the service. There was always this jerk taking your order. He was a very old man, too old to still be alive if you ask me. He had these villain-esque features with paper thin lips and these dark gray eyebrows that curled upwards on the ends. The only real sign he gave you to indicate that he was in fact still alive, was him sniffing hard in his left nostril, which would slightly ripple the skin along one side of his face. Other than that, he was just the mayor of scowl city.

"Whatchu want? Whatchu order now?" The cruel man said. Jesus, settle down, I thought to myself, but I didn't say anything. I never say anything bad to people that serve you food, even if they mess up on your order. Chances are, if they mess up on your order and you *tell* them they messed up and you want it corrected, they'll just fix it by spitting in it and bringing it back to you with a big smile on their face. Needless to say, I am always as nice as I can possibly be when it comes to people handling my food.

"Your order, whatchu want? C'mon." The cruel man said to me again. I wanted to smack him, I really did, but I remained calm and just ordered my food.

"Burger, fries, and a Coke please," I told him. The man turned to the cooks.

"One burger! One Fry! One Coke!" he screamed. He was nuts. After the currency exchange, he gave me the large Coke, and I went and sat at one of the empty tables in the outside covered area. I had just barely sat down when he yelled out my order. I do have to hand it to the place, they were fast. I think the cooks were a little afraid of their lunatic boss too, which made them haul ass on every order.

I sat and ate at the only vacant picnic table. The table in front of me was occupied by a couple arguing. I tried not to listen and just kept my head down while I ate, occasionally looking to my right at the cars passing by, but it was just too damn juicy too not eaves drop. The boyfriend kept telling his girlfriend that she couldn't hang out with one of her friends anymore because her friend was a slut, and every time they hung out together he always had to go pick her up from somewhere shady. The girlfriend was much louder than him and was not having it one bit. Every other word was an F-bomb, and she was telling him she can hang out with whoever she wants to. I couldn't hear every word she was saying, mostly just the F-bombs because every time she said one she raised her voice. I couldn't see her face since her back was to me, but I could see her arms waving furiously and her long curly dark hair was bouncing left and right and forward and back. All I could hear at that moment was, "Blah blah blah, fuck that, blah blah blah, fuck you Steve, blah blah blah, oh hell no, blah blah blah, fuck you Steve!" This went on for a few minutes when suddenly, they both stood up and starting making out. Like really going at it. I was in serious awe. What the hell just happened? I thought to myself. Then, after a few seconds of them locking lips, they held hands and walked away. What the hell just happened? I thought to myself, again.

As they got up and left, I noticed an elderly couple having lunch at the next table over. It was odd. They had an infant with them. I studied their interaction with the child, but they didn't really interact with the baby at all or each other, for that matter. They both just sat and ate their food quietly with their heads down. My mind started thinking of scenarios about these elderly folks. Were they the grandparents and just babysitting for the day? Most likely, I thought. Then my mind *really* started to wander. What if their daughter is sick in the hospital? What if their daughter and her husband died in a car wreck and now they are the guardians? I thought to myself. Could these two elderly folks be the sole caregivers of this child? Or, what if they just adopted the infant? Can people that age adopt babies? That wouldn't seem right to me because then they wouldn't be around much longer to raise the child anyway. Or, what if they had a family feud and they just kidnapped their grandchild and are on the run? You hear about that kind of thing on the news all the time. My outlandish scenarios were quickly stomped out like the heel of a cowboy boot to a cigarette butt when a mid-thirties couple walked out from the diner with food and sat next to the elderly folks. The man in his mid-thirties started playing with the baby, kissing his or her toes and talking baby talk. Obviously, I was a little off since it was quite clear that I was looking at three generations from the same family.

Behind me sat a handful of kids—six or seven high-schoolers I'm guessing. They were loud as hell and laughed like hyenas. Each kid had almost a different hair color—one green, one blue, a light orange, a dark orange, and two girls had the same pink dew. One of the girls had on tight leopard-print pants and what looked like fishing tackle on her face. I didn't mind the way they dressed, though. They were fun to look at. But hearing them say the word "like" almost as much as that girl from before—the one who was dropping the F-bombs—it made me want to finish my burger and fries as fast as I could and get the hell out of there. So, I did.

I threw my empty bag in the trash and stepped out on the sidewalk. The last thing I wanted to do was head back and watch video games and see Terry's ugly mug. So, with my large Coca-Cola in hand, I started walking up Arroyo Parkway in the goddamn rain.

Colorado Boulevard is a very lively place. It's where they have the big Rose Parade every year on New Year's Day. A bunch of bars, restaurants, stores, and a ton of people occupy the two-mile stretch. I figured that would be a cool place to go wander around for a bit on that Saturday afternoon since it was only four or five blocks up.

After a couple blocks, the rain really started to come down and I was getting drenched. A park bench under a giant tree was in my view about fifty feet away. The bench looked dry as hell so I sprinted like a leopard and made my way there. I was soaked. I threw my Coca-Cola in the trash bin and fantasized about holding a hot cup of coffee. The rain was coming down in buckets. My plan was to wait out under the tree and try to dry off a bit, then, make another attempt for Colorado Boulevard.

After a few minutes of watching cars drive by and nearly drowning from the splash from their tires, I started thinking again about the night before and was trying to remember what the hell it was that Harvey had said to me. It was like trying to remember song lyrics, or that actor in that one movie, or who won the Super Bowl a particular year. All things you can just google nowadays, I might add. In most cases, it is better not to think about it and sooner or later the answer will pop up when least expected out of nowhere. Well, I didn't care so much for that method at the moment, and I wanted to know the answer right that second. It didn't work out that way. Not even close. And it was nowhere near the tip of my tongue.

The rain finally let up after about twenty minutes, and I stood up and stepped out from under my friendly tree and made my way up to my destination.

A half-block or so, from when you get to Colorado Boulevard by way of Arroyo Parkway, it begins to incline. Naturally, by the time I made it to Colorado I was huffing and puffing with my hands on my knees, head down, and facing the ground. I finally caught my breath and sort of liked the fact that it was sprinkling since I was a tad overheated. But even still, I hated the rain and would rather have clear blue skies, the sun out, and the day be hotter than hell.

When I lifted my head to gaze on the wild wonder that Saturday's brought to the famous Colorado Boulevard, much to my dismay, it was dead. No one was around. Another problem with L.A. is that whenever a single rain drop falls from the sky, everyone scatters like they are in a minefield. The one street in Pasadena where I could go and have a little fun had just turned into a fucking ghost town.

The rain had let up quite a bit since I had left that bench down by Lucky Boy. I figured, what the hell, and decided to at least walk the two blocks down Colorado to Fair Oaks Avenue, then down Fair Oaks and back to my apartment. I was almost making a complete loop, but it still seemed much more amusing than sitting on my cot in the living room watching Terry roll his cigarettes.

My clothes were completely soaked through as I made my way down the street looking through the windows of the establishments. Some bars had a handful of people in them. Most of them were probably shopping at the clothing stores before it began raining, then decided to scurry inside and have a drink just to avoid being drenched. I'm sure bars make a killing in bad weather.

The stroll I was taking was incredibly boring since there was no one around outside. I felt like I missed the memo on not going to Colorado Boulevard in Pasadena, California this exact Saturday morning.

I was one block down with one more to go until Fair Oaks Avenue, when I heard a faint sound. I decided to search for where it was coming from and right away I knew it was some sort of horn. My ears followed the sound that lead me to the intersection of Fair Oaks and Colorado, where I saw a man sitting in a chair against the wall playing a tuba. As I got closer to him, I could tell he was very old, with weathered leathery skin and more wrinkles on his face than a 25 year-old pug on its death bed. He had on this light brown suede suit, but it wasn't nearly as nice as it sounded. It was noticeably dirty and had a rip in it that went from the middle of his shin all the way down to his shoes, which were these crummy used cross-trainers that had Velcro straps barely attached. But boy, could he play the tuba. I don't really know how a well-trained tuba player sounds, to tell you the truth. But when you are soaking wet, bored as hell and walking through a ghost town, then all the sudden you stumble upon a lone man in a faded suit playing a tuba, it sounds goddamn heavenly.

I stood there and watched him play those quick bubbly notes. He noticed me standing there and stopped playing.

"Hey there, my boy, it's rainin' like a sun of a bitch," The old tuba player said, in his hoarse, raspy voice, almost sounding like he was running out of breath.

"Yea, it is," I smiled and said. "I walked all the way here from South Marengo by Lucky Boy." He adjusted himself in his rickety foldout chair to get more comfortable, and lifted his tuba over his head and laid it flat on his lap suggesting that our quick chat would turn into a long drawn out conversation. I didn't mind, though. It was Saturday, and I didn't have anywhere else to be.

"Those is some nice shoes," The old tuba player said, as he leaned over his instrument and gazed upon my shoes. I didn't hear what he said at first. I was too busy being a jerk and staring at his setup. He had his tuba case open on the side of him with a couple of ratty blankets inside and a coffee cup on the ground in front of him. It was half full of random change.

"Scuse me?" I asked.

"I said those is some nice shoes."

"Oh. Oh thanks," I replied, as I looked down at my tan tennis shoes I've had for months. They looked like crap and hurt like hell. Just the weekend before, I was going to go buy some new ones to tell you the truth, but I put that on the back burner for some reason or another.

"Is they comfortable?" he asked.

"Well, to tell you the truth, just last weekend I—"

"Yea, I bet they is," he interjected. "I bet they's real comfortable. They probably cost you quite a bit 'a money too." The old tuba player pulled his instrument over his gut, and looked down at his shoes, tapping his feet up and down, left foot then right foot, over and over again as he opened and closed his eyes to match the foot he was tapping. He then started singing—mumbling really—in a type of ragtime gospel melody, but his words just *did not* seem to match. "Left foot, right foot, brown bear, black bear, green fish, blue fish, left foot, right foot."

Needless to say, I felt a little uncomfortable standing there listening to his original hit and I began to look around for some sort of onlooker support, but the streets were still desolate. I just accepted the fact that he was a tad bit out of touch with reality and carried on.

"That's a cool song," I said. I was lying, of course. He stopped his ballad abruptly, raised his wrinkled head with his eyes closed, then slowly opened them and made eye contact with me.

"Yea, it's a cool song, but that's all it's ever gonna be." He seemed slightly upset in a way. The light-hearted jovial way that he greeted me with had just turned into a mixture of sadness, bitterness, and just plain sourness. "Songs can't take you nowhere, not a real place, anyway." he said. "You close your eyes, play a song, finish that jam all the way through, then you juss end up in the same damn place you was when you started."

I was done by then. It was just too much crazy knowledge from an old tuba player to a 21 year-old kid on a rainy Saturday in southern California. It was time for my farewell speech. I said goodbye and let him know how much I enjoyed his playing. I dropped four quarters in the coffee cup that was now in his hand, which he was shaking. After I dropped my coins in, he brought his cup all the way up to his eyes to investigate it. He shook it around hard a few times with brief pauses in between, where he would tuck the cup under his left eye and use it as some sort of microscope. I said goodbye to him for the second time, but I don't think he heard me. I started walking away and said goodbye for the third time, a little louder, but he kept shaking his cup full of coins with his left eye practically inside of it. As I was halfway down the block on Fair Oaks Avenue, I heard him yell to me, "Don't forget yo' shoes!" Whatever the hell that meant. But right when the old tuba player said that to me, my brain switched gears and all of the sudden out of nowhere, I remembered. I remembered what Harvey had told me the night before. It came out of nowhere, just like that sudden wave of the cold air-conditioned breeze when you walk into the front doors of the Firm on a sweltering 90-degree day. In two weeks, I was going to Las Vegas.

The night before, sometime between Cameron and I meeting the two ladies—and Cam getting wild on stage—Harvey and I went up to the smoking lounge and puffed on a couple cigars. There was this girl there that started talking with us. Sheila—I think—or Shyra. Something like that. She was this adorable short blonde with dark red lipstick on and these big beautiful blue eyes that took up half of her face. She lived near The Shadow Club and was a waitress at the Voodoo Lounge, which was a small bar just a block up. I can't remember how it was brought up, but she had told us that her and her friends had just got back from a wild weekend in Vegas. That is when Harvey's eyes lit up and told her, drunker than a skunk, that he and his buddies were going there in two weeks and had the hotel rooms and all the other arrangements taken care of already. Harvey then turned to me and told me I should go with them. I said I would love to.

So, long story short, I was walking down Fair Oaks soaked to the bone, in the pouring rain, when I finally figured it out. I was going to Vegas in two weeks. With Harvey. And his disciples. What could possibly go wrong?

Chapter 4

The following two weeks leading up to the three-day getaway were long and rather uneventful. It was just like anything in life when you're anticipating something whether it's a birthday, holiday, a sports game, concert, or even just waiting to get off work on a bad day. Whatever the case may be, time always seems to go slower. I did however, get the invitation and benefit of having lunch with Harvey and his crew a couple times in those two weeks. I wouldn't say it was anything spectacular, nor was I expecting it to be, but it was nice getting to know everyone who was going on the trip just so it wouldn't be awkward when we were there. I'm sure that was Harvey's intention in the first place. Either that or he just invited me to lunch because we got along so well, probably a little of both.

It was the day before we left, a Thursday. Cameron and Harvey arranged for me to stay at their place that night and take off in the morning. Harvey's house was a goddamn palace. I had never seen anything like it, at least not in person. It was right on Manhattan Beach with a million bedrooms and a huge open living room area. In the center was a huge bright red pool table, where you had to walk down a couple steps to make it there. There was a built-in bar on the far corner and not a *single* T.V. *in* the place. Four giant windows faced the ocean. It was like watching a documentary on California beach life through those windows, and with a view like that there is no need for television. You could watch the waves crash behind the volleyball players, children scooping buckets of sand, and babes tanning. You had it all. Skateboarders and beach cruisers weaved around the walkers and joggers on the paved runway that ran along the entire beach and into the next one.

During the house tour Cam gave me, Harvey announced he was off to bed, "It's gonna be a crazy beautiful day tomorrow," Harvey told us on the way to his room, "See you boys tomorrow." Cam and I hollered goodnight and decided to play a couple games of pool, but after a half hour or so with no clear winner, we just decided to hit the hay. Cam pointed down the hall to the room I was staying in and we called it a night. My new "suite" was twice the size of my apartment.

I arose in the morning to the sound of someone trying to wake me up. It's funny how that works. When someone is telling you to wake up, you instinctively know they told you to wake up at least three or four times before your eyes finally opened. It was Harvey.

"Get up you son of a bitch! Do you know what time it is? C'mon ya son of a bitch!" Harvey shouted, in a comical sort of way.I lifted my eyes and smiled.

"Morning, Harvey. No I dunno. What time is it?" I asked.

"It's time to take the bull by the horns, you crazy son of a bitch! That's what time it is! But for real, it's 10 A.M. We've hollered at you for the last hour and a half to come and eat breakfast, but you were sawin' some serious logs like you got in my liquor cabinet last night and drank all my Crown Royal. You stealin' booze from me you bastard?" Harvey laughed. "You always sleep this late?" he asked.

"If I had a choice, ummmmm yea," I said, hesitantly. I didn't want Harvey to think less of me. But I was honest. I could sleep any given day until mid-afternoon. Some say it's a gift, others a curse. I just think it is what it is.

"Well never mind that." Harvey said. "Are you ready? Are you ready to turn that town upside down with your bare hands, you young dragon slayin' son of a bitch?"

"Uh, that's the plan," I laughingly agreed.

"Well get up then. We got some breakfast on the table for you. So take a shower and get ready. C'mon, let's go. I got a suitcase full of liquor, and two coolers that we'll fill up when we get closer to the promise land." Harvey was very entertaining that morning. He was like a kid getting his first squirt gun, and it was contagious as hell. I hopped up, showered, got dressed, brushed my teeth, and ate the two eggs and two pieces of toast on the table all within ten minutes. I loved getting my first squirt gun.

The plan: Harvey, Cameron, and I would pick up Rory, and just meet Paul, Glen, and Barry at the hotel since those three were driving together. We made our way back to downtown L.A. near the firm where Rory's loft was. Rory Carson was a short muscular guy, with spiked blonde hair that he highlighted, and a big toothy grin. He was loud, but not in an annoying way. He always thought before he spoke, and when he did it was a strong booming voice. If you've never seen him before and he was talking behind you, you would turn around expecting the sound to be coming from a guy that stood six-foot-four and two-hundred and fifty pounds. He was always chewing gum too which could totally throw you off. Imagine seeing a short, spikey-haired, toothy-grinned guy snapping his bubble gum. You would definitely think he would have some nasally Joe Peschi-type voice. But nope, this guy sounded like Paul Bunyan.

Rory came out to the car and threw his stuff in the trunk. He hopped in shotgun, which Cameron kindly gave up, and we were off. Through downtown, out to 101, then passed Pasadena where I looked out the window and raised a middle finger, pointing it towards my apartment—particularly to Terry. We passed through Arcadia, then Monrovia, and further east out into the great unknown.

The drive there was just like any other exciting short road trip. Everyone starts out talking really loud about the most absurd things, like how drunk they're going to get, or how many girls they're going to get with. Then after an hour or so, the conversation shifts to old stories—the craziest thing they've ever done, or when they had a near death experience, or that one time in Cabo they woke up sunburnt behind a dumpster with a mysterious new tattoo and their pants down by their ankles. Then, the conversation moves to work talk, which only lasts about twenty minutes because the terribly boring subject of work almost makes the driver nod off. The driver then grabs a cd and throws it in and the remainder of the drive is spent in deep thought and reflection. Then, when everyone notices the road sign that has the name of the destination and the mileage sign showing it's only twenty miles away, the conversation comes full circle and everyone talks at once at the top of their lungs about how drunk they're going to get and how many girls they're going to get with. Yes, this road trip wasn't any different.

I had to admit—driving into Las Vegas at 1 o'clock in the afternoon isn't very mind-blowing. I've seen all the movies where it shows this town at night and was preparing myself to be awestruck, but in the daytime this place looks almost post-apocalyptic. It's out in the middle of nowhere for chrissakes, in the desert, and it's hotter than hell. The first thing I thought was, who in their right mind would decide to build a city here?

We pulled into our hotel, which is at the beginning of the strip. I kind of wanted to drive around the city and look around for a bit, but it wasn't my place to start calling out our agenda for the weekend, so I kept my mouth shut and just went along for the ride. The other guys were already up in the rooms so we checked in, got our keys, and made our way into the elevator. Harvey was pulling two coolers on wheels full of beer that we had picked up a few miles back. A couple shirtless strangers were in the elevator with us and, of course, had to exchange some stupid cliché words.

"Aww, you got me an early Christmas present?" Douchebag #1 said to Harvey, as they both looked down at the coolers.

"Maybe next year, my man," Harvey replied. They both laughed that forced chuckle that strangers always do. It annoys the hell out of me. There was that awkward silence that happens in elevators when you are in one with strangers. But sure enough, once the door opens and you step out, the talking picks up again. That annoys the hell out of me too.

Paul and Glen were sitting on the couch watching basketball on the tube when we arrived at our rooms. They both jumped and gave a loud cheerful welcome as if to say, it's time to party. They were probably just sucking up to Harvey, though. Paul Chance was the epitome of tall, dark, and handsome. He was a total lady's man and loved himself more than anything. He always dressed well and was always overly nice to everyone but in a slimey way, calling everyone buddy, pal, champ, or chief. It was disgusting, but he was always nice to me so I never did him any wrong. It was just his way of going about things that really bothered me. He was one of those guys that would spend more time getting ready than his girlfriend, who he'd cheat on in a heartbeat if he was presented the chance, which he did on several occasions. Then there was Glen Patton. He wanted to *be* Paul. They literally had the same hair, same skin, same build, and he was good looking as well, but he didn't have the same charisma, not even close. He was shy and very genuine. Paul was just cutthroat, simple as that.

Once we looked around the room and set our bags down and figured out where we'd all sleep, Harvey opened the coolers and started tossing beers to everyone.

"Here you go, you bastards. Drink up. Let's get some. R-O-C-K in the U.S.A!" Harvey yelled out. He was truly on cloud nine. "So what's the plan? Hey, where the hell's Barry?"

"Hell if I know," Paul said.

"Yea, right when we got to the room, he left and we haven't seen him since," added Glen. "Did he say where he was going?" Harvey asked.

"Nope," both Paul and Glen said at the same time.

"Well shit, his loss. Looks like there's nothing left to do but drink as much as possible until that rat bastard shows up," Harvey chuckled, as he cracked open a beer, chugged it, smashed it, threw it against the wall, burped louder than a dump truck, and bent down and grabbed another can from the cooler. He looked at all of us noticing everyone in the room had their eyes fixed on him and the hilarious spectacle they had just witnessed.

"'the fuck ya'll lookin' at? Let's drink!" Harvey hollered.

Paul walked over to the table and turned on some tunes from these little portable speakers he brought, and for the next hour we just drank and talked about three topics: girls, ladies, and women.

Finally, the door opened and there was Barry with four bags of groceries. Barry was a timid guy, but you wouldn't be able to tell just by looking at him. He had a wide jaw, jet-back black hair, and sported a chain wallet that hung clear to his knees. He looked like a lean, mean, fighting machine, but was a very passive soft-spoken character. He had recently started seeing a girl in the accounting department who I'd messed around with a few times before, so it was always a bit awkward when he and I conversed. It also didn't help that everyone in the entire Firm knew about it. Drama spread like wildfire on those seven floors. You would always have to try and control your liquor when everyone would be out at happy hour because the next day at work, by 4:30 in the afternoon, all seven floors would know what ensued the night before and how much of an ass you made of yourself. *Trying* to control your liquor and *controlling* your liquor are two different things, though. I was known around the office as "Dirty Quinn" for a few months due to a certain happy hour episode one infamous Friday night in October, though I honestly can't remember the allegations. Luckily, that embarrassing nickname faded and I was simply known as "Quinn" for the rest of my stint. Anyway, so Barry comes back with the groceries and we are all a handful of beers deep.

"Well, well, well. Look who brought us some goodies," Harvey said, as he laughed loud as hell. He thought he was God's gift to comedy. He *was* quite entertaining though, I'll give him *that*.

"Sorry, guys," Barry said. "I just went to get us some things for the weekend."

"Ol' Barry, always prepared. Ah, don't worry about it. Here you go my buddy ol' pal," Harvey told him, as he handed Barry a beer. You could tell the alcohol was getting to Harvey, but not in bad way. He was in a great mood and it was quite contagious and intoxicating—pun intended.

The next few hours were a lost cause, as we stayed in the room and drank like madmen with loud hip hop blaring, courtesy of Paul Chance. Apparently, the plan now was just to hang out in our rooms until it was night time then we would barrel downstairs into the abyss of sinfulness. The clock finally struck 9 P.M. and the music was promptly shut off.

"Alright, alright. Listen up, you stallions and slayers. Times' a wastin'," Harvey announced. "Let's get downstairs and find some women." Everyone rushed into the other room to the closet, where they grabbed their nice button up shirts and sports coats, then made their way to the bathroom where they doused themselves with fifty pounds of cologne. Cameron and I, both drunk and sitting on the couch, were perfectly satisfied in our jeans and simple t-shirts. Paul walked up to us with a green bottle of some sort of stink.

"Stand up you guys," he said. We both stood up—what else were we going to do—and he doused us each with four sprays of some lady killer venom, or so I thought. "There, now you're ready to knock 'em dead," Paul said. I had to admit, whatever Paul sprayed on me didn't smell half bad.

"Alright, let's do this," Cameron said, as he hit his elbow against mine like he was asking for some sort of reassurance from me.

"Sounds good," I replied. "Let's do the damn thing." I was drunk, so my reply was super intelligent.

Just as we were heading out the door, Rory jumped down to the floor by the T.V. and did twenty push-ups. I knew he did exactly twenty because he counted each one out in his strong Paul Bunyan voice, "1...2...3...." He then hopped up and started jumping up and down and kicking up his knees as high as he could, all while chomping on his bubble gum and displaying his big, white, perfect teeth. "Let's get it on," he said, bobbing his head from side to side, each ear to each shoulder, almost as if he was preparing for a cage fight. He finally ended his ridiculous routine and we made our way downstairs.

As I walked out of the room with everyone and down the hallway, I noticed I was awfully Bambi-legged and had a terrible case of shutter vision. Every time I turned my head it was like a click of a camera, and I knew right away I was way too drunk to be going on any kind of adventure. We headed down the elevator, the stench of cologne so strong in that tiny space that I was getting nauseous and started counting down the floors in my head as they lit up on the switchboard—4...3...2...1. The doors split open, and as we stepped out into the nightlife of Las Vegas, Nevada, I gasped for a breath of fresh air, only to be overwhelmed by the clouds of cigarette smoke floating throughout the casino floor.

Chapter 5

The casino was loud with distant crowd cheers—or moans—from people either winning or losing at the craps tables. Sirens and circus-slot-machine-noises were bouncing off each other in the cathedral-esque room full of plumes from cigarette smoke and high hopes. Cocktail waitresses scooted around like wheeled robots showing nothing but cleavage and long legs, as they handed off drinks to every walk of life.

There were the senior-citizen loners sitting at the slot machines who inhaled cigarettes so deep it was impossible to notice any visible smoke as they breathed back out. Those were the people that really depressed the hell out of me. It was as if they were all drinking from the same water source and that source was directly connected to a nuclear waste facility. I saw one guy with a head the size of a softball, another guy with his eyes farther apart than E.T., and an obese woman with her thigh skin rubbing against the back of her calves as she sat on that poor stool pushing the slot buttons, hoping for a jackpot that would change her life forever.

Then, you had the groups of party girls walking around aimlessly, acting drunker than they actually were. They were obviously in brand new outfits, bought on their lunch breaks earlier that week. All the groups of girls I witnessed were always bouncing off each other with no clear leader taking charge of the bunch. It seemed to me like they were all desperately wishing it was still daytime so they could hang out by the pool just to show off their new amazing bodies, transformations achieved by either starving themselves for the last eight weeks or by some new radical cleanse consisting of nothing but consuming cabbage soup and lemon water. All of the groups of girls would either call it a night early due to a lightweight in their posse, puking after her second margarita, or the really wild ones would end up at the nearest club and stay up dancing all night until the sun rose.

Usually in a group or three's, would be the older men. Probably married, somewhat wealthy, and in town for the weekend to play some golf, gamble, and cheat on their wives. I noticed these types of characters numerous times that weekend. They had girls on their laps who were most likely in the same graduating class as their own daughters.

Walking with attitude, all dressed to impress, and stinking of cologne, booze, and lust, would be the middle-aged guys. I guess that's the category we would fall into. Though I have to say, when we stepped out of that crammed elevator and through the breezy corridor to the threshold of the casino floor, all standing a foot apart in a sort of "Flying V" formation, I pictured us as a sequel to Reservoir Dogs.

You could tell Rory let those twenty push-ups go to his head. He was walking with his chest puffed out and his arms away from his sides. Every time a remotely pretty girl was in view, he would snap his fingers and point at her, whether she was walking right passed him or just sitting at a table talking with her friends and not having the slightest clue that a short, spikey-haired scoundrel who chewed gum like he was hammering a nail, was approving of her physical features.

Everyone followed Harvey around the casino as we made a complete loop, just to check things out I'm guessing, and ended up right back where we were to begin with. Harvey had us huddle up.

"Alright, what's the plan of attack?" Rory asked, blowing tiny bubbles of gum and snapping them with loud, high-pitched pops.

"C'mon, guys. Didn't you notice all the chicks were heading to that dance club in the far corner?" Paul said. "I think that's the best option. Either that, or we can all just go do our own thing."

"No, no, you're right," replied Harvey. "Let's go grab some drinks over there and see what's happenin.'"

Paul led the way this time, as he was more suited for the task at hand. He was the kind of guy that went out every night partying until dawn and would still show up to work looking better than all of us. He'd work ten hours then go out and do it all over again. He was an amazing creature in that respect.

I followed the pack, stumbling a bit, as we made our way through the middle of the casino, shortcutting it to the dance club over by the far corner. I felt in my back pocket and realized I had forgotten my wallet in the room. There was no way in hell I was going to hold everyone up so I simply didn't mention it. Luckily, I didn't get carded at the door, but *unluckily*, I didn't have any money either.

We entered the club and it was dark, with loud trance music you could feel beating in your chest and throat. Strobe lights bounced off the walls and pink, green, and orange laser beams cut across the room spreading in all different directions. Every few seconds you would be blinded by some sort of flashing light, but it didn't really bother me. It made me sober up a bit and I felt alert and in the moment. I was feeling pretty alive, to tell you the truth. It was something wild and out of the ordinary for me, even if it was just some stupid corner of a casino that was being used as a makeshift night club.

Paul took charge once again and ordered us all a Gin & Tonic from the waitress, who looked like every other girl *in* that place. The only difference was she had a name tag. I swear every girl there looked almost identical, everything except for different hair colors. Tan orange skin, tight dresses, the same dews, with their hair up off their shoulders and necks, and I'm almost certain that ninety-nine percent of them had lower back tattoos with either a flower, dolphin, or butterfly.

We were served our drinks and stood there looking stupid, all of us turning our heads about and scoping out the scene. There weren't any *real* tables there, just some black cushions that had the look of glorified foot stools. I decided to try one out and Paul sat down next to me.

"So Quinn, I hear you're from Oregon, is that right?" Paul asked.

"Yep, good ol' Oregon," I replied.

"I'm a transplant myself," he told me.

"Wait, what?" I asked. "You're not from California? Like originally?"

"Hell no. No way," Paul said, "I'm from Iowa."

"Iowa?" I asked him, in a surprising tone almost as if I was mocking his home state, though I was honestly just in utter shock from what I had just heard. Paul can't be from Iowa, I thought to myself. He has all the characteristics of a guy who is L.A. born and bred. He's a womanizer, loves money, and loves looking at himself more than a body-builder does.

"Yea, Iowa," Paul explained. "Moved out here after law school 'cuz I couldn't stand the cold winters. And the girls out here are smokin' fine. Now I'm just living the dream, ya know?" Paul then raised his drink. "Shall we toast? To two dapper young gentlemen from the middle of nowhere. Cheers Quinn." I raised my glass and instantly thought of my boss's one-liner.

"Yessir. I'll drink to that," I said. After I tossed back my drink, I noticed a girl over in the corner by the DJ's table looking at me. She was beautiful. I mean, she still looked like every other girl there but every girl in there was beautiful, so if you're lucky enough to have one of these beauties looking at you, you'd be a pretty happy camper.

I've never been a shy guy when it comes to talking to girls and I wasn't going to start now. Plus I already had quite a bit of liquid courage in me which would've done the trick on its own if I had been too nervous. The key was to make a good impression, at least that's what my dad would always say. Whether it be at a job interview, meeting co-workers, or that first time on the playground making friends, my dad would say a good impression is the key to getting somewhere in life. At that moment, I was aiming to get somewhere alright—somewhere with the brunette in the corner.

I walked over and asked her name. It was Hannah. I would've asked her to dance but the DJ kept playing this terrible trance music that was clearly suited for people who were on something made from only household chemicals you'd find under the sink.

We started chatting away. We weren't really chatting, though. It was practically yelling since it was so damn loud in there. I never understood why drinking establishments had to be so loud. Do they not want people to talk to each other? I'm sure there is some middle ground they could find where the music is loud enough and yet, the music is quiet enough for everyone to converse.

Anyway, she talked my ear off for a while about how she was a nurse from Dallas and how all her friends are here for a bachelorette party. She was cute. Every time I would nod my head in agreement with her, she would open her eyes wide like she was watching a crazy explosion in an action movie. She would also nibble on the straw of her fruit drink she had in her hand, something with cranberry juice it looked like. Her nails were painted perfectly with a pale purple. She was marvelous. I was just about to ask her if I could buy her a drink when I realized my wallet was still up in the room.

Moments later, Paul walked over and introduced himself. What a piece of shit. In a matter of seconds, she completely turned her attention toward him and they both began to have a grand ole time. I stood there like an idiot, not being able to hear their discussion thanks to the DJ. I didn't really want to hear what they were saying anyway.

I turned back around to the guys, but they were nowhere in sight. The club wasn't very big so it only took me a few glances around the place to realize they had split. I turned back around to the two love birds and asked Paul where they went.

"Oh, don't worry about it," he said. "They all just went somewhere else. Probably went to play Blackjack or something. Just you and me tonight, dude. You've met Hannah, right?" I couldn't tell if Paul was being a smartass when he asked me if I had met Hannah or if he was just too buzzed to remember. In any case, I thought I'd entertain myself so I shook my head.

"Nope," I said. "I haven't met Hannah. Hi, Hannah. I'm Quinn. Everyone just calls me Quinn." You should've seen the look on her face when I shook her hand. We had *just* went over this a few minutes prior. She looked at me like I was a nutcase. It was priceless. Serves her right.

Hannah had a friend that was standing a few feet behind her who kept smiling at me. I figured what the hell, so I walked over to her and we instantly hit it off. Her name was Charlene. And although she looked just like her friends and was also a nurse from Dallas, she seemed a bit different, much more grown up. She swore like a sailor, which would usually shoot down the "grown-up" theory, but when she cursed she was good at it, with no sign of it being forced in any way. It sounded like she had been dropping F-bombs since she was a baby and I found that rather endearing. She was awfully cute and sort of easy too. A couple drinks later, which she bought thanks to me being a dumbass and forgetting my wallet, we left the casino to go back to her room.

We were walking outside in the warm mid-March air, when we rounded the street corner near her hotel and were confronted by "Rooster." We didn't know who the hell this guy was, but he sure told us. He was insanely tall, like six-foot seven or so, a dyed red mohawk, and a missing front tooth. He also had that face where you couldn't tell if he was twenty-five or forty-five.

"Hey you guys looking for a party? The name's Rooster," he told us.

"Ah, no thanks, dude," I said. "We're pretty much done for the night." I noticed Rooster was acting fidgety. His teeth were chattering and he kept scratching is upper right arm.

"Oh, c'mon man," he said. "Coolest party in the world. Free booze, drugs, girls, you name it." It was an awkward situation and I could tell Charlene was a bit nervous, so I told him no thanks, for the second time, this time with a smile, and we began to walk passed him. Rooster put his hand on my chest and pushed me hard as he stepped back and reached into the left pocket of his baggy parachute pants.

I've never actually seen a real handgun before, but when he pulled out that shiny silver pistol I knew it wasn't a toy. It looked heavy as he pointed it at my chest, struggling to keep his skinny wrist from bending.

"Give me your fuckin' money," he commanded. Charlene instantly started crying and freaking out. Don't get me wrong, I was scared as hell too, but I was fucking drunk. My slight shutter vision—I think—helped with the intensity of the situation.

"Dude, settle down," I said. "First off, I don't have my wallet. I left it at—"

"Shut the fuck up. Give me your fuckin' money."

"Here, take it," Charlene sobbed and said, as she handed him her purse. Rooster ripped it out of her hands.

"What about you?" he asked me, as he looked around antsy, and about ready to bolt.

"I told you," I said. "I forgot my wallet at—"

Rooster pushed me aside and sprinted off passed us around the corner and off to hell, I hoped.

"Are you alright?" I asked Charlene. She was shaking terribly.

"Oh my god, oh my god, oh my god, oh my—"

"It's okay," I told her, "It's all over now." I tried comforting her with a hug, but she loosened her body and slipped through my arms. I stepped back to give her some space as she paced around, shaking her hands vigorously in front of her.

"Oh my god, did that just really happen?" she asked, in one big panicked breath.

"Are you okay? I said. "Can I help you in any way?"

"No. No you can't. I'm sorry. I just need to get back to my room."

I offered to walk her to the front desk of her hotel, and she agreed. It was the least I could do.

No phone numbers or mailing addresses were exchanged. We just went our separate ways. An episode like that can be quite heavy for some people, obviously heavier when you *aren't* drunk.

After we said goodbye, I went back outside and took an evening stroll. I was awfully buzzed, and Paul was really starting to get on my nerves, so returning to the club was out of the question. I had no idea where Harvey and the rest of the gang was. Despite not having my wallet, I had my room key in my pocket, so I stumbled back to my room, shutter vision and all, and called it a night.

I laid down on the bed fully-clothed, kicked off my shoes, and began to doze off. As I laid there, I realized something funny. I realized that Charlene will always remember me, even though it was due to that scary encounter. Even still, she will always remember Quinn Kershaw for the rest of her days. It was shallow to think that, but hell, no one can stop their own thoughts. She'll always remember Rooster too, for that matter. You got to hand it to ole Rooster, though. That son of a bitch sure knew how to make an impression.

Chapter 6

Sunlight streamed in through the window causing the temperature to be well into the triple digits. The stench of day-old hops cursed the room's interior. Socks, shoes, and shirts were all scattered aimlessly on the floor, draped over doorknobs and the backs of chairs. An ironing board was set up with three red plastic beer cups on it, two standing upright and one on its side with no actual iron to be found. It was the morning after, and I had a hangover for the ages.

My head rattled as if there was popcorn popping in my brain but instead of regular kernels, a handful of BB's, or worse even, jagged rocks. I felt like someone had shoved a rigid arrowhead through the top of my skull and the wider my eyes would open the more severe the pain. My mouth was dry and felt as if it were lined with that pink fluffy house insulation. The rays of sunlight piercing through the window and onto my ragged face didn't help a goddamn thing. Lying there fully-clothed, I studied my surroundings and noticed the room resembled a frat house more than a hotel room.

We had three rooms all connected by a door in between each one. I sat there on my bed hunched over, my eyelids low, trying to buffer as much head trauma as possible. The T.V. was on in the other room but the volume was so low I couldn't make out what was on. Who cared. I sat there for a half-hour or so trying to conjure up a series of somewhat simple thoughts, but my brain pounded so hard that I just kept still and stared frivolously into the abyss of the striped design on the hotel wallpaper. Some time had passed when I finally entertained an idea, and it was a good one. Why don't I get my lazy ass up and see who else is in the rooms or at least see what time it is, I thought to myself.

I pushed off with my skinny arms and stood for second, Bambi-legged, then instantly plopped back down onto my behind bouncing once on the bare twin bed, the sheets and covers scattered on the room floor. Light-headiness tingled my skull causing the room to appear moving, and I had to re-coup.

The hangover blues played its melody in every exhausted corner of my body and I was depressed. I missed The Dalles. I missed the cool fresh air that breathed off the Columbia River. There were two hills near my hometown that were grassy and looked like the butt cheeks of a giant laying on his stomach. They led down to the river and often in the summertime I would picnic on those hills. I would eat and drink and then stroll down the giant's backside to the opening of the valley that lead to the water's edge. I wish now more than ever I could be there. I wish I could wash my face and baptize myself a new man, a sober man. I wish I could just lie there on my back, hands nestled behind my head, refreshed by the water's chill, and listen to the tune of the birds and the soft breeze rustling through the leaves of the Albus trees. I wanted to be there so bad I dug deep in my mind to find it. I lied back on the bed, arms behind my head, closed my eyes, and attempted to picture my Heaven on Earth. It was unsuccessful. The pin-point pounding of a knife blade touch was cutting deep in my forehead, stabbing back through my eyelids to the pulsating rhythm of my heartbeat. But I was determined.

You must get to the mini-fridge and find cold water, soldier, I commanded in my head. I was the lone survivor on an unforgiving desert planet and my only chance for survival was getting to that fucking mini-fridge.

I took a few deep breaths, and with one eye squinting like a pirate—my attempt at balancing the pain to just one side of my head—I pushed off the bed with my new military-sized arms and stood. It was successful.

Hobbling across the room, I made it to the fridge and found two chilled bottles of water staring directly at me. I saw them as shiny bars of gold and it was 1849. After I gulped the second bottle down, I hadn't realized I had already finished the first. I let out an "Ahhhh," like in a Coca-Cola commercial and made my way back across the room in my 99 year-old body, stepping through clothes and bed sheets to close the blinds and block the scorching sun from my sorry face. There on the window pane, sat my goddamn wallet. It was, of course, neighbored up to a red plastic cup half-empty of warm beer which made me want to throw up. I forced myself to calm my throat glands from flapping all about and ejecting stomach lining as if I was Linda Blair in The Exorcist. Fortunately, after a few deep breaths, I didn't have to release the hounds.

Glancing out the window, I was instantly blinded by the beaming yellow sun, but through my squinting I could still make out the crowded streets and high-rise buildings that were all jumbled together on a sweeping grid. The metropolis stretched for miles then began to dissolve and finally die out into a desolate desert wasteland.

I closed the blinds and something remarkable happened. Everything seemed better. My pounding headache was still present, but besides that and the minor T.V. noise in the other room, the new darkness cooled the place down and made an ambience no hangover remedy could do. I tried to further this new "better" feeling by turning the air-conditioner on that was just below the window, but without it having a simple on/off switch, I was confused by all its various colored buttons and was going cross-eyed by the thought of reading some manual to figure the damn thing out. It would have no doubt caused me to suffer a nervous breakdown.

In the same room as the T.V., a grumbling from the coffee maker sounded. I hobbled in to see who was awake, but there wasn't a soul in sight. On top of the T.V. sat a clock. It read— 2:40 P.M. Holy shit, I thought to myself, I guess it's not morning after all. The sunlight was pouring in through the "T.V. room," so I did as I had done in the previous room—drew the blinds and closed off the wretched sun to welcome the beautiful life-saving cold blackness of a dark room.

I plopped down on the couch and just as I did, the phone rang. The phone sat on an end table that was butted up against the couch and when it rang inches from my ear, the loudest resonance I had ever heard cried out. Was there an invisible someone jiggling around a kitchen knife that was stuck dead center inside the top of my face? I thought. I stayed as still as possible and just barely reached my arm out long enough behind me to pick up the phone. Keeping my eyelids as low as possible, damn near closed, I answered.

"Hello?" I asked. It was Cameron.

"Dude, why aren't you down here? We're down by the pool," Cameron said.

"Um, I think I'll be out of commission for the next few hours. I'm hurtin,' Cam. Where did you guys go last night?" I replied.

"We left the club after we saw you and Paul talking to those girls and just went and played blackjack for *hours*. We got back to the room and you were passed the hell out, thought you were dead, man," Cameron laughed. My hangover was suddenly turned up a few notches, and I had to hold the phone a few inches from my face as Cameron's voice felt like a vibrating needle jamming into my ear canal. "What did you do last night?" he asked.

"Well, I was pretty drunk and I—"

"Yea, I could tell," Cameron interrupted. "You slept in your clothes, Quinn."

"Yes, I am aware of that," I embarrassingly replied. "I met this girl last night, the one at the club," I was honestly too hungover to explain the details of the story. It was making me nauseous, to tell you the truth, and I had to cut it short. "And we were walking back to the hotel room and we got mugged. So, yea, we just called it a night."

"Damn, really?" Cameron loudly asked.

"True story," I confirmed.

"Hey guys, Quinn got mugged last night!" Cameron hollered. I could hear them all gasp in the background, obviously shocked. "You okay?"

"Yea, luckily I was quite intoxicated so it didn't really freak me out, but a different story for the girl," I said, in a weathered, tired voice. "I feel awfully bad for her."

"Jeesh, Quinn. Yea, that's too bad," Cameron said. "Well at least you're both okay. Anyway, get your ass down to the pool when you can and tell us the whole story. My old man rented a couple cabanas, there's chicks everywhere." He *did not* have me at drinks.

"Alright, I'll be down there soon," I said. I lied. Hanging up the phone, I made my way into the bathroom to pee and drink a glass of cold water. I stripped down to my underwear and laid on the couch in the T.V. room. Now with the blinds closed, the room cooled down considerably. There in the dark, I sat and watched a Michigan State vs. Penn State girls' basketball game. I would've changed the channel, but with no remote in sight, getting back up was on the back burner of my things to do. I didn't want to move a single bone in my body. It ached too much.

Two hours had gone by and the *last* thing I wanted to do was leave my security blanket—my dark shaded dwelling. To be honest, I was awfully embarrassed that I had slept so far into the day, so I figured it was time to get move on and finally face the world.

Clumsily donning my yesterday's outfit of jeans and a dark blue t-shirt, I made a quick pit stop to the bathroom to splash cold water on my poor weathered mug. I leaned down and took a pull right from the faucet like a dehydrated St. Bernard.

As I left the room and made it down the long hotel hallway, the elevator doors shuffled open just before I could push the button. "Gooday mate," a man said, as we passed each other by and switched places. He was dressed in full firefighter attire. Medium stature, square-jawed, GQ-looking, and well-built, this man in his thirties carried a small piece of paper in one hand and a boom box in the other. As the doors began closing, I reached my arm out to re-open them and find out just where this fire *was*. I could see him looking down at his scrunched-up note then bob his head back up towards each door as he moved down the hallway, searching for a particular room. He made his way down fifty feet or so when I had to, once again, keep the elevator door from shutting, using my foot this time. Once he found his destination, I watched him knock on the door, the door opened, then listened to him speak, in his Australian accent no less. "I heard there was a fire. Is anyone in need of medical attention?" A gust of female screams and giggles burst out from their chambers and a woman's arms reached out and reined him in by his red suspender straps—a male stripper fireman. I smiled and shook my *still* pounding head. Only in Vegas, I thought to myself, as the irritated elevator doors finally closed on me.

Chapter 7

Entering the lobby, I noticed the guys right away. They were hard to miss, still suited in tank tops, shorts, sandals, and all of them displaying a new layer of bright orange skin resembling a troop of vacationing lobsters. They were standing by the front hotel doors, the big clear glass ones that lead out to the u-shaped parking lot. It was lined with taxi cabs and new arrivals. Despite looking like absolute clowns with their new tans, they were all acting normal, except for Glen. He was hammered. He was *beyond* hammered.

His eyes were barely open and his left arm hung loosely around Paul's neck, Paul trying to help him with his balance. Glen turned to me.

"Hey, maaaan, I know yoooou," Glen said to me, in his slobbery speech.

"Lookin' good, Glen," I said, in an asshole sort of way. I don't know why I even said that to him, let alone in that tone of voice. I guess I was just moody and pissed off at myself for being achy and miserable and had no one to blame but myself. I mean really, who was I to talk? I had just been hiding for the past ten hours like some depressed cat lady.

"You arrre tooooo, Quinny Quinn Quinny," Glen slurred.

"Alright you sons a' bitches," Harvey commanded, as he leaped forward in front of us all and clapped his hands a few times like he was our football coach, "time to slay some dragons." Harvey then instructed our taxi drivers on the location of the restaurant we were heading to. Paul might have had a few moments of leadership within our clique twenty-four hours previous, but Harvey was clearly back in charge *tonight*.

We loaded up in two separate cabs. I was with Paul, Glen—lucky me—and Barry. The location of the place was only a few miles away but while in route, it was just long enough for us to get booted out from our means of transport.

"Are you a gooooood driver there? Huh Mr. Taxi mannnn?" Glen asked, barely keeping it together.

"You're damn right I am. And you better shut up, kid," the driver said, in a stern, annoyed tone. He was an older man with white hair just past his shoulders. His face wore deep wrinkles, like miniature cable lines going every which way from the top of his hairline and down his cheeks. His hands were locked at "10 and 2" as he was intensely focused on the road. Judging by his black jean vest that had a few random patches stitched on it, I knew it was no coincidence that Van Halen was sounding from the cab's stereo. The only thing that was missing were those knuckle gloves that drummers wore in the 80's. I didn't really want to judge a book by its cover, but I could tell this man had some miles on him. He either played in a rock band way back when or was a roadie for one. And his constant nail biting and short fuse convinced me he was either an addict or in recovery.

"Hey driver, yoooou can't drive," Glenn slurred. "You drive like an ol' mannnn. Noooo, like an old lady," Glen chuckled. "Yea, you are an ol' lady." Glen sat further back in his seat, leaning his head all the way against the head rest. The driver looked furious as he squeezed the steering wheel, turning his knuckles white.

"Chill out, Glen," Paul commanded. Paul was sitting up front in the passenger seat turned around toward us, trying to keep order. "Just cool it, we're almost there," he said. I was next to Glen and squeezed his knee, an effort to have him calm down a bit. He didn't take the hint.

"Quit tryin' ta be a perv, Quinn," Glen said. "You're tryin' ta feel me up, ain't cha Quinny? You perv, man. Hey driver, you're an ol' lady."

"You better shut up, kid," the driver warned. As he drove on, he ruggedly massaged the back of his neck, making it clear he was beyond wound up but still trying to soothe his irritation. Glen *would not* keep quiet, though.

"A leather jacket? Who wears a leather jacket?" Glen said, teasing the cabbie.

"Alright, that's fucking it," the driver yelled. He stomped on the brakes and we flew forward into the seat in front of us. We were pushing around 40 MPH, so when he hit the brakes, we skidded a damn near whole block. "Get the fuck out, you fucking punks!" he shouted.

"How much do we owe you?" Paul asked.

"Are you being serious? Are you honestly being serious with me right now?" he said to Paul. "Just get the fuck out. Free ride tonight, ladies." The driver was *irate*.

We scurried out of the cab like pigs out of a chute, then I turned back to help Glen from the vehicle. He was slow and clumsy, but I managed to get him out and standing on the sidewalk. The cab driver appeared out of nowhere, standing directly in front of us, and without hesitation, he threw a hard punch and his fist met solidly into Glen's stomach. Glen immediately fell. The driver stood over him for a second with his fist still clenched, contemplating whether or not to stay on the attack, or perhaps he was standing his ground in case we were to jump in in our friend's defense. Paul, Barry, and myself threw in the white flag and raised our hands high as we all silently agreed Glen deserved it. The cabbie finally loosened his tight fist and stepped over Glen and around the car. He drove off as we kneeled and huddled around Glen, who began puking.

Somehow, Harvey and the others were nowhere in sight. Our driver was so erratic and speedy that we lost sight of them somewhere along the way. Either way, it was fine because we all knew our destination—Corrina's Steakhouse.

"Well now what?" Glen said.

"What do you mean?" I replied. "We'll walk to the restaurant and meet the rest of the guys."

"Let's make sure Glen's all right, then take it from there," Glen urged.

"Well of course," I said.

"Man, screw going to the restaurant. Glen, get up. Let's go somewhere else. I know a killer spot," Paul said. He forcibly picked Glen up, hooking his foreman under Glen's armpit and pulled. "C'mon Glen," Paul said. "Get up, let's go." Paul was just an arrogant ass. Glen slipped through Paul's grip, like a bag of leaves tearing through the bottom of a sizeable plastic garbage bag. He landed hard on the grass strip that lined the sidewalk and threw his guts up for the next ten minutes.

"Go somewhere else, Paul?" I said. "What are you even talking about? We are meeting Harvey, Cam, and Rory at Corinna's Steakhouse. That is the plan. Deal with it."

"Deal with it?" Paul mocked at me. "Who the hell are *you*? We'll do whatever the hell I *say* we're gonna do."

"What about you, Barry? You cool with this?" I asked. Barry shrugged his shoulders like a coward, glanced at me, then pointed his eyes down, embarrassed at himself. Barry sure resembled a tough son of a gun with his chiseled physique and chain wallet, but boy was that guy a sissy.

Glen finally stood up on his own. He began speaking and I noticed his slur was hardly noticeable. Wow, that taxi driver must've punched all the booze out of him, I thought to myself.

"Okay, here's the deal," Paul commanded, "let's say to hell with dinner and go raise some of our *own* hell. I literally know a spot less than three blocks from here. Shall we?" No one said anything, all of us just stood there like weaklings. "Okay then, here we go," Paul said, as he began walking and we began following.

Exactly three blocks later we were standing in front of a small, black, square building, lined with pink neon trim and bright electric palm tree signs attached to the outer front siding.

"Here we are, boys. Shall we?" Paul said.

"What is this place?" I asked. "There's no name outside."

"That's what makes it so cool, Quinn," Paul replied. "This is the Pink Door." And sure enough, the two front doors were painted pink.

We approached the entrance and a giant bald bouncer in a green suit greeted us. He opened the door and said good evening. Paul, Glen, and Barry proceeded in, but I refused. I asked Glen if he wanted to join me to wherever I was going, due to the shape he was in, but he laughed off my invitation and displayed a drunken grin. His loyalty and admiration for Paul was so immeasurable that I actually felt sorry for him. Who would want to hang with Paul? I thought to myself, let alone *be* like him.

"Take 'er easy, Quinn," Glenn slurred to me.

"Yea, see you tomorrow, probably," Barry added.

"Sounds good, Barry, and you too, Glenn," I replied.

As we said our goodbyes and went our separate ways, Paul shook his head at me in disgust. I didn't care, though. I knew I was on the right side of history.

The guys stepped into the club as I began strolling the sidewalk, not quite sure what to do at that moment. I contemplated just waving down a cab and hitching a ride to Corinna's Steakhouse, but Paul poisoned my every ounce of being and any chance of optimism flew out the window the second he started bullying Glen and jerking around with Harvey's plans. I was pissed off and alone, and I wanted to be.

A sudden whiff of Mexican food surfed in the air, my stomach growled like a Grizzly and my appetite began to make all the decisions. The scent I followed was just to my right, directly across the street from the Pink Door. Smack dab in the middle of a run-down vacant parking lot, was a glorious shining silver taco truck. It might as well have had a halo above it. With the smell of grilled pork dancing in the air and into my nostrils, I grabbed four delicious street tacos and on my merry way I went. I strolled into the mid-March evening with no destination or reason to have one. Waves of different groups passed by as I walked along, feeding my hungry soul arguably the greatest meal of my life. I noticed a family of four, with a husband and wife and two small children—a boy and girl. The kids were no more than six or seven years old. The little boy and girl were each nibbling on a hot dog in one hand and holding a balloon in the other, as their parents followed behind them taking pictures of the sights. A few feet behind *them* stumbled three inebriated college girls bound together by interlocked arms. Loud and proud, they were performing their drunken swerving version of Follow the Yellow Brick Road. "We're off to see the Wizard..." the girls sang, as they skipped in a loose zig-zag formation, almost breaking the ankle of the tall one in the middle—damn heels. What kind of parents would take their six-year-old children to Las fucking Vegas for a family vacation? I thought to myself. Was Disneyland *that* much more expensive?

A few blocks later, I decided to take a side street, an alley, really. This street looked broken, an overlay of potholes and voids where puddles with the glimmer of neon city lights would reflect off if it had not been for the dry-as-hell weather swallowing every ounce of water in sight. There were half as many establishments and street lamps on that particular block as opposed to any other area I had been. Adjacent from my path, across the first intersection, was one of those Vegas wedding chapels. What struck me was the reader board. It was the exact same one as the church I grew up in. Except for this one read: "SAY I DO. IN THE ONE AND ONLY LAS VEGAS. BY THE ONE AND ONLY KIND OF ROCK N ROLL. ELVIS PRESLEY." The sign was pearl white with a wavy blue floral border, *just* like the one at home.

For a moment, it took me back to Sunday mass with my mom, dad, and big brothers, Scott and Torey. It also reminded me of our pastor. Pastor Len was tall, loud, bearded, and funnier than hell. His sermons were always cautionary tales and always rather long, but never snoozers. His wife, June, was a short heavy-set lady with freckles and quite the opposite of her husband in the socialite category. She was a sweetheart and always had a kind thing to say, if there was ever the offbeat chance of you hearing her get a word out. Their two young daughters would sometimes set off the entire congregation in an uproar of laughter as they would blurt out a "Hi daddy" or "Daddy, I'm hungry" during one his sermons, squirming and fidgeting next to their mother in the front pew. Molly and Milly always had on little matching plaid dresses to go with their pigtails, but by the end of the church service would resemble a pair of ragamuffins, each one missing a shoe and wild-haired, like they had just stuck their hands in a light socket. I hadn't thought about the Potter family in quite some time and deep down it made me feel guilty.

I was cold to the bone now, amidst the hundred-degree heat. That nostalgic feeling was setting in, like memories from my youth—riding bikes around the neighborhood with my best friends or spending my annual week in the summer with my grandma and grandpa, where my grandma would buy me things my parents never would—a cap gun and sugary cereal came to mind.

Walking briskly along and trying to keep myself warm, my hands shoved deep in my pockets and my chin tight to my chest, I spotted a bright green light flickering on the street corner ahead. I finally got close enough to make out what it read: "SID'S PAWN & GUN."

This pawn shop shared a parking lot with a strip mall consisting of the usual nail salon and teriyaki businesses. It was its *own* building though—beige-colored, with chipped paint and veiny cracks throughout the exterior, like a dried-up riverbed.

Pawn shops are always a treasure hunt in themselves, so I figured taking a look inside would be a fun way to kill some time. I really had no place to be anyway.

As I approached the front doors, a man and woman were standing there just to the right, leaning against the building wall. I didn't want to judge a book by its cover, but the duo looked shady as hell. He had slicked-back dark brown hair, and had on a black leather jacket that went just past his knees. The faded blue jeans he wore were filthy and unwashed. His lady friend, a prostitute I assumed, was taller than him, just over six feet. She was the typical bleached-blonde, with a set of double D's that literally took up one-third of her body. She—barely—had on this leopard-print tube skirt, which exposed her vanilla-pale legs that had noticeable cuts and scratches on them. She was smoking a long thin cigarette and her hand was shaky as she pulled it toward her face to take a drag, hiding under seven pounds of makeup.

"What the fuck are you lookin' at, chief?" the man said to me.

"'Scuse me?" I replied. Now I'm not one to ever start a fight, but I'm also not one to ever back down from one either and the series of events on this trip so far already put me in a pissy mood. My heartbeat sky-rocketed in an instant and I b-lined it straight toward the hot shot as my fists and jaw tightened. As soon as I was just steps from his smug mug, he cowardly moved backward along the wall, tripping over the foot of his bimbo companion and grabbing ahold of her fluffy white poodle-haired-looking purse to keep himself from falling. "I was just kidding, chief," he said. His tone was that nervous, joking around-type voice. I'm sure he had that same feeling you get when you flip someone off in a car who just cut you off, then the car slows down to confront you in mid-drive. You have that "Oh shit" feeling of instant regret.

"Not so tough anymore?" I replied.

"It's all good, I swear. All good, my man. Okay?" he said, as his voice cracked. He put his hands up in surrender and just as he did, I noticed his girl eyeballing him up and down with a squinted face and open mouth. I could tell she was disgusted from how much of a whiney sad excuse for a man he was. What I found truly funny though, was that him picking a fight with a *complete* stranger was okay with her, and even maybe sexy, but backing down from a fight, now *that* was something just embarrassing. Miss Fake Tits disgusted me more than Big Mouth did.

The whole ordeal lasted no more than thirty seconds, but in that minute window of time, I had envisioned a scenario where I actually went through with it. As I clenched my fist back behind my shoulder, twisting my torso, I summoned all the strength and worthiness my thighs and hips had to offer and I drove my bare knuckles through his deserving cheek-bone. Blood squirted and splattered from the wise guy's face like a blown gasket off an overheating Chevy Bel-Air on the side of a desert highway in the middle of summer circa late 1950's.

Unfortunately, Sid's Pawn and Gun was an absolute hole, and after a mere three minutes of making my way up and down the aisles, trying my damnedest to find something on the half-empty shelves interesting enough to hold my attention—I'm not going to stand there and fidget with a dinged-up old guitar amp—I decided it was time to move on down the line.

When stepping out from the same doors I came in, I was glad to see that the creepy couple was nowhere to be found. It's the little things.

The sun was setting and the blood-red sky faded into pink, then orange, then a brownish yellow. Directly above me, you could make out two faint shimmering stars poking through the vast canopy of dark blue. As I stared up at the awe-inspiring natural wonders of the universe, my moment was ruined by the strong smell of car oil and dumpster trash and the constant hum of traffic noise, either up close or from afar, but always there, that suffocated the mega urban sprawl in the middle of nowhere.

My night had already seemed to have started on the wrong foot, and with my body still in recovery mode, I waved down a cab and called it a night.

Chapter 8

The swift sound of a zipper woke me up. It was 10:21 A.M *exactly*. I know that for a fact because the moment I opened my eyes, I noticed the bright red digit lights of the alarm clock on the nightstand staring back at me. I sat up on my elbows, eyes squinted, not quite ready for the day. I could see Harvey opened his luggage and was rummaging around until finally pulling out his swim trunks.

"Good morning, my boy," Harvey cheerfully said. "It's a beautiful day out, time to seize it, Quinny. By the way, any good stories from last night? We lost you guys."

"Not really," I said. "I ate some good tacos, though."

"Is that right? Well now, we'll have to go check that place out. So, are you liking Vegas?" Harvey asked.

"Yeah, it's pretty cool so far." I said. I was lying though. That soulless town was everything that I was not.

"Is this your first time here?" Harvey asked.

"Yes it is," I said, as I yawned and stretched my arms out high and wide. "How about you, Harvey? You ever take Cam here when he was little?" As soon as I asked that, Harvey's whole demeanor changed. His smile straightened out to a blank stare. He pushed his thin lips together, as he was searching for the right words to say.

"You and Cam sure have hit it off," Harvey said in a less cheerful tone than before. "It took *us* a lot longer than you two to become friends."

"Huh? What do you mean?" I replied. I sat up on my behind and rubbed my eyes hard, forcing myself to wake up faster than my body was ready for. I had no idea what Harvey meant by his cryptic message and I was determined to get to the bottom of it.

"Well," said Harvey, "Cameron and I aren't your typical father and son combo. His mother and I only dated for a few months, years ago, when I lived in Chicago. Cam was raised by her and been living with her until about a year ago, when he moved down here with me. To tell you the truth, I had never even met him until then." Harvey began his speech smiling and carefree, but halfway through he sat on the edge of the bed, gazing out the window, his words slower, but stronger and deeper in tone. "I would just send him birthday cards and Christmas presents," he said, "and maybe another thing or two over the years. Hell, I can't even remember." Harvey sounded ashamed. He looked down at his twiddling thumbs and the room stood silent. Harvey looked broken. He was slouched, his back hunched over like a child in timeout knowing they had done something wrong. I wasn't sure if I was to change the subject or if Harvey was in some sort of self-therapy and needed to get this off his chest. "And you know what else, Quinn?" He had never called me Quinn before. Always Quinny, or Quinny Boy. "Cameron was the one that wanted to come here and live with me. Not me. He called *me*. I should've been the one to call, Quinn." Harvey's voice was noticeably shaky and for however awkward the moment was, it was quite a spectacle to witness a grown man owning up and accepting his own defeat. It was beautiful, actually. Harvey continued, still staring down at his crossed hands, "So when he called, it was a feeling I will never forget. Like a weight had been lifted. I felt like I was—"

Bam! Suddenly, the door burst open, interrupting Harvey's intimate testimony. In stumbled two loud men, Paul and Glen—laughing, cursing, and drinking. Yes, the two-man circus was in town and we had front row seats. Harvey freaked.

"Get the fuck outta' here, you motherfuckers!" Harvey yelled. Silence. The room was so quiet you could hear an ant tip-toeing across the carpet. Glen was startled, turning instantly sober and standing at attention before his commanding officer. But not Paul.

"Calm the hell down, Harvey. This is Vegas. Try and have a good time." Paul said, in the slimy and condescending way that only Paul Chance could do. The sheer arrogance of that guy would make anyone want to punch him square in the nose, for no other reason than that. "Jeesh, Harvey. Blah blah blah. You need to take a pill," Paul said. "We get it. We interrupted your little pow-wow with the mailroom kid. What were you two hacks talking about anyway?"

"That's it!" Harvey yelled. Harvey stood up and looked demon-possessed, with his face beet red and a vein popping from his neck. I had never seen him like this. "I'm going to ring your goddamn neck, Paul, you little punk!" Harvey stepped toward Paul and thrust his arms out in hopes of doing what he had just said. I sprinted out of bed and wrapped my arms around Harvey to contain him.

"Fine, fine, we're going, we're going," Paul said. He was trying to play it cool, but it was obvious that he was quite shaken from Harvey's actions.

"And *mailroom boy*? Really, Paul?" Harvey said, irritated, but calmer now. "His name is Quinn and he's better than you. He is better than *you*, Paul. You hear me?" Harvey's voice got louder and louder, and was in a full-on shout by the end of his comment.

"Oh, is that right?" Paul answered, shouting back.

"Yes, he is. In fact, why don't you and Glen just grab your things and go?" Harvey said.

"We are." "No, like grab *all* your things and leave. For good. I paid for these rooms, and now I want you to get the hell out." Paul froze. He stared at Harvey to see if he was being serious. He was.

"Wow," Paul said. "Fine, we're gone. C'mon Glen, grab your stuff." Glen showed a slight hesitation, trying to decide what to do. He looked at Harvey and me, then at Paul, finally deciding to follow Paul, his hero and look-alike.

The next five minutes were incredibly awkward as Harvey stood staring out the window at the buildings and weekenders downtown. Paul and Glen were noisily packing their bags in the next room over. We could hear Paul huffing and puffing and barking out quick shouts of bitter cussing. Glenn was quiet, though, and just doing as he was told. They finally left the room the same way they came in—loud, and with a big slam of the door. The circus had left town.

"Well that was fun," Harvey said, as he turned to me, laughing, and shrugging his shoulders. His smile was short-lived though, as he turned back toward the window. Rather than him looking down upon the city, he stared down at the floor, his thoughts still wrapped around the conversation we had before Tweedle Dee and Tweedle Dum barged in. I knew this was something that would not easily pass. "Come on," Harvey said. "grab your trunks. Let's go down to the pool and forget about all this." I smiled and nodded.

"Sounds good," I said.

Chapter 9

An annoyingly loud sound system blared around the pool area. The DJ was dressed in an orange tank top with matching shorts and long dreadlocks wrapped up in a bun. He stood behind his table on the far corner of the pool spinning records of the latest Top 40—Mariah fucking Carey, *again.*

A couple hundred people half-naked occupied the pool and the outlying area. I laid flat on my back in a lawn chair nursing a frosty cold Heineken, resting it between my hands on my stomach. I tilted my head forward to observe the scene, but all there was worth watching was a few pretty girls in bikinis and a couple of white pillowy clouds changing form against the clear blue sky. However, I *did* begin to notice Harvey drinking stiff drink after stiff drink and becoming more and more agitated.

It was just him, Cameron, and myself at that point. Barry and Rory joined Paul and Glen back to L.A. I couldn't tell if Cameron noticed his father's behavior, but *I* sure as hell did. Cameron sat in the lawn chair next to me doing pretty much the same thing as I was. Harvey was standing across the pool from us, yapping with some "new friends" of his. I noticed he would chat loudly with them, then laugh hysterically, then moments later right back to a straight face, almost to a frown.

Even from that distance away, I could tell he was thinking about something, his brain wrapped around a thought that he couldn't let go of. Every five minutes his glass would be empty and he would walk the twenty feet over to the outdoor bar and grab another one of his favorite drinks—a double Pendleton whiskey. I observed this for about an hour or so, when I dozed off under the hot sun.

I woke up startled by Cameron shaking my shoulders. Surprisingly, I was asleep for an hour and still managed to not spill my now *warm* bottle of Heineken.

"Get up, Quinn. C'mon, time to go." Cameron said. He talked fast and sounded annoyed.

"Why? What's up?" I replied.

"It's my dad. He wants to go. He's drunk and mad and talking all sorts of crazy. He wants to leave right this second back to L.A. Come on, we gotta go grab all our stuff." Cameron told me.

"Thought we weren't checking out 'til tomorrow," I said.

"Yes, I know that, Quinn," Cameron said, rolling his eyes. "My dad just wants to go. Like now. He's already up in the room packing. We'll grab our things too and I'll go get the car. My dad said he'll meet you in the lobby and I'll pick you guys up outside the lobby doors, got it?" Cameron said. I sat up and rubbed my eyes and yawned loud. I was slightly confused because for one: I had just woken up and it took me a moment to even just realize my own name, and two: I thought Harvey was having the time of his life. Why would he want to leave? I thought to myself. Did any of this have anything to do with what he said to me in the hotel room earlier? I bet it did. I kept my opinion to myself and followed Cameron through the crowd of drunkards and partiers, feeling a new slight suffocation on my skin. I was sunburnt. Apparently, snoozing under the unrelenting rays of the Las Vegas sun can do that to a person.

After Cam and I finished packing, we left the room and split up so he could grab the car and I could go get Harvey from the lobby. Leaving the living room, I turned around for one last look. I was embarrassed. Our room looked like a cyclone had hit it. Beer cans and plastic cups scattered everywhere. Smashed crackers and chips smooshed in the carpet, and that damn ironing board still folded out in the middle of it all.

As I made my way down to the lobby, I passed a group of guys just arriving that I *swear* were our body doubles. Was I in a parallel universe? I thought to myself. Was this group about to do the *exact* same things that we all did for the past seventy-two hours? The youngest one in the group even looked like me, with his crew cut and sporting Wayfarer sunglasses. One of the men—the "Harvey" of the group—in his early fifties and wearing what looked like a million-dollar suit, was toting a cooler on wheels. There was no way in hell I was going to make some typical indirect frat boy remark about the contents inside and how cool I thought that was.

When I reached the lobby, I came upon Harvey scrunched over in a chair, his head down between his legs. I knew he had been drinking quite heavily, but I could still tell that something was wrong.

"Ready to go, Harvey?" I asked. Harvey slowly lifted his head and moved his squinted eyeballs in each direction until he spotted me.

"I'm a terrible father," Harvey said. He put his head back down between his legs and repeated his previous comment. I stood there like an idiot, because I had no clue what to do. Luckily, I could see Cam parked right outside the lobby doors waiting for us. I helped Harvey up with my hand, hooking it under his armpit, and escorted him to his car. He plopped in the backseat and literally within a minute, he was asleep. I didn't mind at all though, I got to ride shotgun.

"Time to go," Cam said, sarcastically, laughing at his sleeping father. I don't think Cam even realized that Harvey wasn't feeling well. I just kept it myself though, as we made our way out of the city of sin and toward home.

I nodded off for a bit on our way home. It was easy to relax in the brand spanking new jet-black Mercedes, equipped with all the bells and whistles, one being a state-of-the-art air conditioner that could put a baby to sleep—as it did to me. We were just about to the state line near Primm, Nevada, when I heard a low grumbling just behind me. I turned my head and noticed Harvey's hand over his mouth, foam seeping out between his fingers. He was lying flat on his back, staring wide-eyed toward the sky and looking panicky. His chest popped up like he was seizing, but he was still able to speak.

"I'm so depressed. I'm a son of a bitch," Harvey said. His voice was muffled under his hand-covered mouth.

"Dad?" Cameron yelled. Cam stretched his neck and peered in the rearview mirror to see his father in the back seat. He adjusted the mirror downward to get a better view of Harvey, who was squirming all around and couldn't keep still. "Dad? Dad, are you alright?" Cameron yelled. I could feel the car nudge forward, Cameron's foot unknowingly pressing the gas amidst the chaos. Harvey removed his hand and wiped the drool from his cheeks. He wasn't foaming anymore, but he was extremely agitated and breathing heavy and hard.

"I'm sorry I was never there for you, Cameron. I'm sorry. I should've been there. I'm such a loser. Your father is a loser," Harvey coughed out.

"Dad, calm down. Dad, please," Cameron pleaded, as he traded his focus back and forth from the road to the mirror, watching Harvey. "What do we do, Quinn?" Cameron asked me. Cam kept switching from using both hands on the steering wheel, to one hand on the wheel and the other scratching his thigh in a fast, nervous motion. I thought for a second, then said the first thing that came to my mind.

"Turn around," I said.

"What?" Cam replied, surprised.

"Turn around and we'll go to the hospital, the E.R." I said. "We are closer to Vegas than L.A., so just turn around and press on the fucking gas!" Cam looked expressionless, trying to decide. "Cameron!" I yelled. "Turn the goddamn car around!" *This time*, without reply or hesitation, Cam slowed down just enough to bust a left and drive through the gravel median in between highways. Once we were straightened out and heading back toward Vegas, Cam punched the gas pedal and drove those next thirty miles going a hundred and twenty miles an hour. I looked back at Harvey and he had his hand back over his lips, but no foamy spit spewing out this time. He was mouthing something, but I couldn't make out what.

"Harvey, how you doin' back there?" I asked. I reached my left arm over the seat and rested it on his knee cap, hoping to at least comfort him in any way possible. He didn't respond. He was still just staring up. I couldn't tell if his low-voice speech was intended for Cam and I, or if he was talking to himself. I leaned in to try and decipher his words through his mumbling.

"...Give us this day our daily bread, and forgive us our sins, as we forgive those who sin against us..." he mumbled. Oh no, I thought to myself, he his reciting the Lord's Prayer for chrissakes. I quickly straightened up, putting myself firmly back in the passenger seat and turned to Cameron.

"Hurry up," I told him.

"I'm trying, Quinn. I'm going as fast as I can."

"Go faster!" I shouted back. From my door, I could adjust every window in the car, so I lowered the backseat windows a couple inches. "Is that better, Harvey?" You want more of a breeze back there?" I said. I was trying *anything* to make the situation better. Harvey gave me no response. Cameron was driving like a bat out of hell now, but we had no choice. Weaving in and out of the other cars, he would dip his shoulder into each slight turn of the wheel.

"C'mon, C'mon, out of the way!" Cameron yelled. "Move it! Get the hell out of the way! Dad, you doin' okay back there?" No response, just Harvey still staring upward.

Almost to Vegas but still stuck in the car, it was the most helpless feeling ever. I reached my arm back again and rested it on Harvey's leg. The least—or most—I could do was let him know he wasn't alone.

"Quinn," Harvey whispered.

"Harvey, you okay?" We're almost there. We're gonna get you some help," I said, as I started to cry.

"Cameron," Harvey said, able to speak louder than a whisper this time.

"Dad! Dad, I'm going as fast as I can! Hold on!" Cameron called out.

"Cameron, if I die I want you to know that I love you, son. I should've been better. I am sorry, Cameron. You are my son and I love you," Harvey said, in a mixture of crying, coughing, and aching. It was the saddest thing my eyes had ever seen.

"You're not gonna die, dad," Cameron cried. "Dad, you are not gonna die, you hear me?" Cameron's voice turned from light crying to all-out sobbing. He reached his right arm back between the two front seats. Harvey grabbed ahold of Cameron's hand and they held on to each other for the remaining seven miles, finally making it back to Vegas and pulling into Mountain View Hospital.

The parking lot was surprisingly scarce, and we were able to drive right to the front entrance. I leapt out of the car and sprinted so fast that I had to wait a second for the sliding glass doors to open. I turned my body sideways and squeezed through the doors as they began to open, screaming, "Help! My friend is dying of a heart attack! Help! Somebody please help!" Two nurses—a man and woman—ran toward me and followed me out to the car. The man peered in the window and without hesitation, ran back inside and brought out a wheelchair. Cameron and I stood off to the side, helplessly watching them load Harvey up into the wheelchair as he coughed, shivered, and hyperventilated. They wheeled him back inside the sliding glass doors where the female nurse explained to us that they would be with us shortly and for us to sit in the waiting room. I looked over her shoulder and watched Harvey being wheeled down the long white hallway, through a set of flapping doors, until he was no longer in sight.

Chapter 10

We sat in the waiting room for an hour. Cameron was sitting up in his chair, his legs shaking uncontrollably as he bit his nails, staring off into the blue and white stripes of the hospital carpet. The doctor finally came in, and as he approached us in his white coat, gray hair, and black-rimmed glasses, he avoided eye contact. I knew something was wrong. Cameron and I stood up.

"Which one of you is Harvey Gans's son?" he asked.

"That's me," said Cameron. The doctor continued.

"I hate to be the one that has to tell you this, but your father has passed on. I'm truly sorry." My stomach sank. I was waiting for Cameron to either burst out in tears or screams, but not Cam. He stood there in front of the doctor for a few seconds, calm. "If there's anything we can do for you, don't hesitate to let us know," the doctor said.

"Thank you, sir. I appreciate all you did," Cameron told him. I myself was clenching my jaw and stomach, trying my hardest not to cry, which made it even worse. The frog in my throat turned to a lump, then the lump turned into a sand-papery mountain and I had to let it out. I gasped loudly and fell back down in my chair, my face in my hands, balling my eyes out. I could feel Cam's hand on my shoulder comforting me.

Why is Cameron comforting *me*? I thought to myself. It should be the other way around. He just lost his father for chrissakes. I wiped my tears away and stood back up. I gave Cameron a hug. I wanted him to know I was there for my friend, but deep down, I knew he was the one comforting *his* friend.

"I think you need to come with me," said the doctor to Cameron. Cameron nodded then turned to me.

"I'll be back in a little bit, Quinn. Just wait here," Cameron said. He followed the doctor behind closed doors to make the necessary arrangements for Harvey.

The waiting room was like a sick joke—people sitting in uncomfortable hard plastic chairs, reading magazines, trying to ignore the fact that they soon will be on the receiving end of some very bad news. Elevator jazz bled from the overhead intercom trying to lighten the mood, but all that ivory tickling and soft blowing of the saxophone did was torture you.

A middle-aged lady to my right buried her face in the latest issue of People Magazine, as her two young children ran around like chickens with their heads cut off. There was a woman seated directly in front of me who had to be in her nineties. She was thin and gaunt and sat alone, with only an oxygen tank to keep her company. Her bald head was covered with a purple handkerchief. She smiled at me as she adjusted her seating position, noticeably uncomfortable and in pain.

The only thing I wanted to do was be home, in Oregon. I wished I was 12 years-old again, seated at the kitchen table with my mom, dad, and two brothers eating homemade pancakes and fried bacon. After breakfast, we will load up in my parents' blue minivan and head out to one of Scott and Torey's baseball games. There, I will sit next to my dad and be young and naïve and he will explain to his son the rules of the game. Somewhere in the middle of those nine innings, I will ask my old man for some money, and I will scurry over to the concession stand and buy popcorn, a soda, and a licorice rope. I will sit there on the bleachers in between my mom and dad, happy as can be, watching my big brothers field and catch and throw. The crowd will roar as a homerun is hit and the player rounds the bases. I jump up and cheer with everyone else, as I gaze up at my taller than life parents. But I wasn't there. I was among the sick, and the crying, and the dying, and the weak, and the tragic, and the despairing, and the miserable, and the burnt-out broken and lonely people of the desert.

With a few quarters I had stuffed in my wallet, I stepped outside the front entrance of the E.R. to use the payphone. I called my mom. When I began dialing the number, I tried to convince myself I could hold it together and just tell her I was calling because I missed her, but the moment she answered the phone and I heard that familiar genuine voice of my dear mother, I broke like a glass vase thrown onto solid rock. I wept loud and explained all that had happened and told her that I loved her and my father very, very much. Our bittersweet conversation ended and I hung up the phone.

I went back inside and sat in the waiting room for another hour when Cameron appeared and explained to me that he had to stay. I obviously understood. I offered to stay, but he insisted I fly back and he would catch up with me in a few days. We hugged and said our goodbyes. I was crying, but Cameron remained strong. It was such a remarkable thing to witness. A 21 year-old kid being so bold and grown up in such of moment of suffering and loss.

I took a cab to the airport and grabbed the first flight back to L.A. When I *arrived* at the airport, just outside the first outside entrance, was a homeless man. Unlike the old tuba player I encountered weeks before in Pasadena, this guy was not much older than me, maybe even younger. He was filthy and sitting on a bucket, playing a trumpet. Next to him, was a little make-shift bed for his cat—a blanket covering a wicker basket. In it, a little paper bowl that was half-empty with cat food. I'm not sure what song he was playing, but it was the saddest tune I had ever laid ears on. I reached in my back pocket and gave him the fifty-seven dollars I had in my wallet.

The plane ride home was only forty minutes, but it felt like forever. My stomach ached with sadness. As I peered out the airplane window and over the vast desert of the American southwest, I wondered where Harvey was now. Was he some-where in the air, somewhere in the middle of all this space, watching over us? But it was too soon for those thoughts, and all my heart and mind could acknowledge was pain and regret. Regret that I didn't say something to Cameron about Harvey's condition before the car ride home.

When I finally made it back to Los Angeles, I was going to call Cole for a ride, but I knew Terry would have tagged along and the last thing I needed at that moment was an hour-long car ride with Terry yapping about nonsense. On the *cab ride* home from the airport, the driver was friendly and tried to start small talk. He asked me things like how my night was going and how I liked living in the city and so on, but I kindly let him know I wasn't in the mood for chit chat. I stared out the window, upon the glowing city lights and pondered many things. What was Cameron doing right now? What is it going to be like at the Firm after this? What are Paul, Glen, Barry, and Rory going to say? But mostly, can I just wake up from this nightmare?

I got home and it was late, sometime around midnight. Luckily, Cole and Terry weren't home. I wasn't ready to explain what had happened. Not yet anyway. I tossed my bag on the floor, kicked off my shoes, and lied down. It was there in the dark that I had one of those "what does it all mean" moments. Why did Harvey even enter my life in the first place? Was this the whole divine design from the beginning, for me to move down here and have *this* weekend happen? A part of me was telling me I barely knew Harvey and that I will be over this in no time. The other part of me was saying that he was a true friend and this will hurt for a long, long time. The latter was winning. I did however come to the conclusion that we are all born, then we all die, and we never know when either of those will happen. Harvey had slayed his last dragon. His 51-story was over now. Now it was up to others to keep his story alive until it eventually fades from history, just as it will happen to every one of us.

I tossed and turned and tried to clear my head so I could get comfortable enough to rest. Finally after a while, I was able to cry myself to sleep on that old run-down cot in the living room.

Chapter 11

The traffic was horrific. It was Monday morning, back to work, and my route was filled with countless car horns and barking and screaming fits from road rage, displayed by commuters. Their heads would pop out their driver's-side windows to shout out words they wouldn't say to their mothers.

Walking up the front steps to the Firm that overcast morning, the building had no resemblance of a flawless Roman temple anymore. It appeared dirty and faded. I eyeballed countless cigarette butts smashed into the hot cracked pavement. I noticed old wads of gum implanted so hard into the granite walkway that they must have been there for a thousand years.

Stepping into the crowded elevator, I was greeted by sad looks from some and a pat on the back from others—attempts at consoling me, I assumed. News traveled fast at Wilson & Hammer Law Firm in downtown Los Angles, and my less-than-24-hours-ago weekend getaway was no different.

I thoroughly contemplated pushing the 9th floor button. I pictured myself stepping off the elevator there and heading straight for Paul Chance's office. I would bust his door down off its hinges with one swift kick, then round his desk and slap him. Not punch him, but slap him. A guy like that doesn't deserve a punch. I would slap the smirk right off his face and stand there and watch him tear up. But I didn't. I pushed the button for the 7th floor. We were all packed in there like sardines as we climbed to our respective floors. Tina Bertner and Mary Chamberlain were in there with me, chatting and laughing about an episode of a T.V. show they both watched over the weekend.

As I stepped off onto the 7th floor, I noticed the light-gray Berber carpet had dark stains. Was it always this dirty? I thought to myself. I rounded the hallway and there at the end was the flickering overhead light that no one had ever bothered to fix. I headed toward it and observed the hallway walls. They were bare—no framed pictures or interior décor. Nothing had changed, it had always been that way, but that was the first time I had *really* taken notice. I stood there, under the flickering light of the empty, ignored, dismal, haunted hallway, and opened the door to the mailroom. Just another day in paradise.

Acknowledgements

To Adelaide Books, for publishing a story I've wanted to tell for quite some time. To Lanakila, for reading the roughest of drafts and not telling me I'm crazy. To David and Jordan, for always listening to my ideas and tearing them apart, with sarcasm. To Matt, for being my connection between this life and the other. To Feliks, for being an inspiration of what an artist is and how they can live a life of purpose. To Josh, Jake, Jeb, Jordan, and Janna, for doing much cooler things than me before I was born. And to Jeb again, for telling me to write this story in the first place.

About the Author

Joe Sneva is a singer/songwriter from the Pacific Northwest. He tours and plays shows under his two groups: "Joe Sneva," and "The Mountain Flowers." Joe resides in Mount Vernon, WA, located 50 miles north of Seattle. This is his first novel.
Instagram: @joesneva
Website: www.themountainflowers.com